the time tower

"Why were we going to sleep up there?"

"It's a Time Tower, Rafferty. We'd be staying at a higher elevation than anybody in the neighborhood. We'd be able to get older than other kids. You know what elevation is, don't you, Raff?"

"You've got this all figured out, haven't you, Larry?" Rafferty says to me.

"Oh, sure," I say. "A Time Tower. The higher the older."

"Is that why all the kids around here sleep in the basements?"

"Yep."

"And every time you climb a tree, you get older?" Rafferty, like any kid, has a high tolerance for things he doesn't know, but here he gives Witt a real long look as if to say, "And what else do they do on your home planet?" Then he says to me, "He's your friend."

the speed of light

RON CARLSON

HarperTempest

An Imprint of HarperCollins*Publishers*

Parts of this book appeared in different form in the following publications:

Journals: *Carolina Quarterly, Ellipsis, Missouri Review, Sports Illustrated, TriQuarterly, Utah Holiday, Western Humanities Review*

Newspapers (as part of the PEN Syndicated Fiction Project): *Our World (The San Francisco Chronicle Sunday Magazine), Northwest (The Oregonian)*

Books: *New Stories from the South: The Year's Best* (Algonquin), *In Our Lovely Desert* (Signature), *New American Fiction* (Hakusui-sha-Japan), *Editors' Choice III* (Bantam), *Best of the Missouri Review* (University of Missouri Press), *Complements* (McGraw-Hill)

The author would like to thank the Utah Arts Council for support and the community at Arizona State University, which has proven great company these many years. This book would not exist without the tenacity and affection of Gail Hochman; it is a novel that benefited under the astute hand of Ruth Katcher.

This is a work of fiction. The characters, incidents, and dialogues are products of the author's imagination. Any resemblance to actual events or persons, living or dead, is entirely coincidental.

Library of Congress Cataloging-in-Publication Data
Carlson, Ron.
  The speed of light / Ron Carlson.—1st ed.
    p.   cm.
Summary: Twelve-year-old Larry spends the summer before junior high school with his best friends, Witt and Rafferty, playing different forms of baseball and discovering the secrets of the universe.
  ISBN 0-380-97837-7—ISBN 0-06-029825-1 (lib. bdg.) — ISBN 0-380-81312-2 (pbk.)
[1. Best friends—Fiction. 2. Friendship—Fiction. 3. Baseball—Fiction. 4. Experiments—Fiction. 5. Family life—Fiction. 6. Coming of age—Fiction.] I. Title.
PZ7.C21678 Sp 2003   2002010982
[Fic]—dc21   CIP
                                                                              AC

Typography by Lizzy Bromley
❖
First paperback edition, 2004
Visit us on the World Wide Web!
www.harpertempest.com

To my sons, Nick and Colin

And to my friend David Kranes

"It's just a world; we can figure it out."

—Witt Dimmick

"I still don't see why you had to call our folks."

—Steve McQueen as Steve in *The Blob*

part one

JUNE

1 the frisco two-step

The history of dance shows it to be deeply intertwined in mankind's social customs. There is a natural urge to move in rhythm to music, but dancing can also be a powerful and effective method of communication. In worship it can be full of symbolic gesture, and in courtship it offers people the chance to get to know each other.

We have dancing fifth period with Mr. Compton, and all year the bigger kids have been moving me up or back in the line when they see where the girls are situated against the far wall. Ivan Kidder and Tim Torkelson arrange the boys' line so they can dance with Karen Wilkes and Linda Aikens and Josie Herron, the cute girls, girls with boobs. In June, we go to dance for the last time, and I notice that Kidder and Torkelson move other kids, but not me. When they get to me, they move somebody else around me, nodding at me or saying "Hi." Something has happened, and I realize that a signal has been exchanged and I could belong with them. They move my buddy Rafferty, whom they call Four Eyes, but they don't move me. Raff hasn't been wearing his glasses for a month, but you can still see the marks on his nose, and the guys still call him Four Eyes.

I look to the back of the line where, as always, the last guy is Witt Dimmick. The last five guys don't get a girl; they have to sit on the folding chairs by the phonograph. This is exactly Witt's plan. He sits there, arms folded, shirt untucked, the way it has been untucked for the six years he's been my best friend. I can see him eyeing the assemblage with a frown. He thinks of himself as a scientist, an observer, but when I ask him about dance class, he only says, "Human behavior. Man, that is trouble."

We have done some stuff. Witt and Raff and I have gone deep into physics and chemistry and electromagnetism and gravity and geology and magic and baseball in its thirty versions, and we have come out the other side. We have done all the experiments you can do on train tracks. We have smashed organic and inorganic matter. We have done experiments with the river. We've sawed a baseball exactly in half with a broken crosscut saw. We've burned ourselves and made ourselves sick. I've puked off the walk bridge down by the junior high twice after our experiments. Raff has puked once. We've only done one experiment with a cat. The cat gave Witt the scratch I can still see coming out of his hair and down his forehead now. I've torn up two pairs of Levi's and one school shirt, and melted the bottom of a shoe. We've done a dozen experiments with household chemicals, and Witt gave Rafferty a tattoo of Utah on his chest that is fading real slowly. He also spelled his name in his big dog's hide with Turtle Wax and bleach. It was a little hasty on his part, because everyone who sees the dog calls it Witt, and its real name is Atom. Witt's motto, which I love, is "It's just a world; we can figure it out."

Things are changing. Torkelson and Kidder are about to be thirteen, out of baseball and after girlfriends. Rafferty and I will be playing our last year of Little League. Witt is going to want to do experiments all summer. He says his goal is "to find out everything. I don't want to know just part."

When the boys' line curves forward to meet the girls' line, I find myself with Linda Aikens, one of the cute girls. There must be some mistake, but no one does anything about it. Her hair is combed and she wears a straight blue dress. Linda is smiling a little, and Ivan Kidder says to me, "Whoa, Larry, way to go." Something has happened.

Mr. Compton nods at Keith Gurber. Keith sets the hi-fi arm onto the record, and the music starts, an old-time song called "The Frisco Two-Step," and Linda and I commence dancing. Witt has his arms folded and watches me with massive disdain.

"What are you doing this summer?" Linda asks me. We've been instructed in the elements of dancing, and after you get three steps into the music, you can initiate conversation. My right hand is on the small of her back in the proper position, and my left hand holds hers out and away to steer us.

It is the boy's responsibility to initiate conversation, but she has jumped the gun. "Play baseball," I tell her. Though I would like to tell her about some of the stuff we've done, the geothermal pit or the crossbow, I know I couldn't make it understandable without confessing that I puked or got caught or got hurt. I wouldn't mind showing her the scabs on my knees; they make it look like I've been somewhere.

"Are you going over to the tennis courts at all?"

There are a couple of seconds between everything we say because I'm trying to keep the two-step beat and steer us clear of twenty other couples. If you lag, Mr. Compton calls your name and begins to clap the rhythm so you can stop "dragging your backsides." If you don't initiate conversation, he yells, "Why aren't you two having a conversation? Have you fallen in love?" Mr. Compton is ominous and riveting in the way of some adults; his long face never moves while he talks. His lips ripple in jolts, as if he is being run by someone standing nearby with a controller.

"I'll be in the park a lot," I tell her.

"Maybe I'll see you there," she says with no delay.

"The Frisco Two-Step" is a spirited number, a song I kind of like, and this is a lot of talking to go with such a tune.

I don't say anything for a few minutes, just steer us around so that we're not facing Witt and his smirk. I can see Rafferty and Cheryl Manwaring headed for the wall, and she's trying to pull him back before they crash. They dance like two people trying not to drown.

I'm quiet right to the end of the song. Linda and I let go of each other, but before I can bow and say, "Thank you for this dance," she whispers to me, "I moved in line to dance with you." Her face looks something, hurt maybe. I don't know what to say, so I just go up to the front and sit. Things are changing as the sixth grade closes down. Why on planet Earth would someone change in line to dance with me? That's got to be insane, and there is no one, not Witt, not my parents, I can ask about it.

I want and don't want to see Linda Aikens at the park tennis courts this summer. I want to hang out with Witt, even if it makes me puke. I want to be a boy; I'm getting good at it. Now Ivan Kidder sits down by me and says, "Nice work. She's a babe." I watch my best friend Witt wander the floor looking for a single girl. He looks like a molecule in the science film we saw last week. He's the last one, and Mr. Compton has begun to clap, saying, "Mr. Dimmick, if you please." The last single girl is Cheryl Manwaring. She's ten inches taller than Witt and she's on his trail now, winding through the room. When she catches him, Mr. Compton will once again signal Keith Gurber to put the needle onto the record and start the music.

We have a tough moment that afternoon when all the girls leave class and see a film in the auditorium with their mothers. It is the weirdest deal so far. At the same time, the boys gather in Mr. Compton's classroom for an informal session. That's what Mr. Compton says: "This is just an informal session."

"What the hell is that?" Raff whispers to me.

"And we can talk about any elements of hygiene you'd like to discuss."

Ivan Kidder and Tim Torkelson laugh a little, their deep, knowing laughs, and the rest of us sit squirming. They used to be kids like us, but now Witt calls them the girl chasers. He says, "Once you start chasing girls, your chances of figuring out the world absolutely disappear."

I actually liked Ivan two years ago. We spent part of one summer hanging out with him. He had a secret club, and we met in his garage and sat on paint cans and talked all day about the password. It was Bluebird. So then we tried the password for a while, sending somebody out to knock on the side door, and Ivan would say, "What's the password?" and the kid would say, "Bluebird," and we'd let him in, and we'd all sit on paint cans. After we did that for half an hour, Kidder said, "We'd better change the password." So we changed it to Redbird, and we sent somebody out to try it. That was the deal with the secret club: we never did anything except talk about the password. Witt gave it up first, and when I joined him in the park, he told me, "That's all they're going to do is change that password. They're through Blackbird and Yellowbird by now. We've got other things to do." Then we went to his house and started digging the geothermal pit.

"Are there any questions about grooming or health?" Mr. Compton says now. I can see the hair blooming from each of his nostrils, a feature that makes going up to his desk in algebra a trial. Of course, no one says a thing. He goes on to talk about hair on our bodies, our voices, maturity, and genitals. The last word he says real low and fast at the end of a ten-ton paragraph. Two days left in elementary school and they pull a stunt like that.

After school, Rafferty stops me and says, "What was that about?" Behind him I can see all the girls and their mothers drifting out of school in pairs toward their cars. They all look down, serious and brave, as if burdened by some new grief; they walk away as if from a state funeral.

"It's all whacked out," I say.

"No, he said what? 'Genitals'? He said 'genitals'? We've been going along all this time and now we've got genitals?" Rafferty, whom I have known since he moved into the neighborhood with his mother and little brother five years ago, makes a face loaded with fear and wonder. He squints at me. "I heard Compton say 'genitals.' How many you got, because I just got the one."

This kind of stuff makes me hate school. Why can't they just leave it at Cuba and the Wright brothers and the ant farm and the Vocabulary Cabinet and Stephen Foster?

I look at Rafferty, with his pale eye sockets, and tell him to forget it, to meet me at the park for some Over the Line. There is a chance, I think, that baseball can still save us.

When we were nine, Rafferty, Witt, and I went down to the park and tried out for Little League. Rather, Raff and I did. Witt took one look at the sign-up table, the boxes of uniforms, and the squadrons of boys lined up for drills, and he got back on his homemade bike. The front tire is half the size of the back, and the seat is from an old pedal tractor. "None for me," he said. "I'm not doing anything where you wear a uniform." He's a good ball player, perhaps the best of us. By dark that day, they'd done all the choosing, and I made Romney Service, the Blue Hats, sponsored by Romney Janitorial. Rafferty was assigned to Boxner Ironworks, the Red Hats, a team coached by Keith Gurber's father.

That summer we watched one kid take over the whole program, Parley, who is the greatest athlete any of us have ever seen. He runs like a cat, and he can hit like a demon. He was twelve that year, and he hit twelve home runs, a league record. It was doubly amazing in that no one gave him a decent pitch. The coaches instructed all their pitchers to walk him and the kids tried to, but Parley hit a lot of outside fastballs over the right-field fence. He is a tall, dark-haired kid with a scar on one ear because of an accident he had with a bomb. He lives somewhere down by where the tracks cross the river, but no one knows for sure. His parents never came to the games, and the rumor is that he doesn't have any. Though he is three years older, fifteen now, he goes steady with Karen Wilkes from our class. She's very pretty, but every time I see Ivan Kidder or Tim Torkelson jockey in line to dance with her, I wonder why they would risk their lives for a four-minute two-step.

The next day school lets out for summer, forever really. We sit around and have the thick chocolate milk and cookies, and then instead of a spelling test or vocabulary, we stack our readers on Miss Miller's desk in two columns, and she opens the door to the playground. This is it. "Good luck with junior high," she says. Every other day I have run through this door and dashed around in the open air, but now I wait a second and then step out of homeroom, past Miss Miller. She pats my head for the last time, and I stand in the strange light of the rest of my life. Witt is gone; I can see him running away, already the person farthest from Edison Elementary.

I've never really had anything end before, not like this. I shuffle along the playground fence. The summer opens before me like an unknowable thing, without law or limit, and I want to go back into Miss Miller's class. I had just barely figured out sixth grade. I walk all the way home up Bowman's alley, and with each step I say, "Last day, last day." If Witt were here, or Rafferty, they'd straighten me out: I should be saying, "First day, first day."

2 ferguson lives

As bioscience has advanced, death has assumed new, increasingly precise and specific definitions. Clinical death is differentiated from somatic death. Death is confronted by most laypersons with ritual or religion, which removes it from the known constraints of the natural world.

Five days later at practice I play a hot grounder at second base, lucking out on a short hop, and I make the throw to first in plenty of time. It's my sixth grounder in a row, and Mr. Robbins, our coach, tells Max Starkey and the other kid behind me to trot out to center field. I've won the position and will play second again this year.

Playing the infield is about keeping your mitt on the ground. When in doubt, you put the fingers of your glove right on the ground, and you stop the ball. You must always make the stop. Witt taught me all of this two or three years ago. A wicked grounder will only hit you in the face 10 percent of the time. It mainly hits you in the arms or the chest, and you can pick it up and still make the out.

After practice, I wait for Witt to show up. He said he'd meet me down here to play Fence Tag or Wall Ball off the old bandstand, but he's nowhere.

I pedal two blocks to his house, my favorite ride in the whole world. Leaning my bike against the old car in the driveway, I call his name and then enter the house where the screen door used to be before Budd, his father, ripped it off and threw it onto the roof. The house has suffered. Budd is an account representative, which is a salesman, for Double American Paper Company, and he keeps odd hours. When his big, red Buick is not in the front yard, it is safe to be around. I go down the stairs, one missing, into the most dangerous, dark place I know, a basement like a landslide, like a train wreck, the teeming depository for everything Witt's father has broken for years without end. If you don't bleed before you climb out of Witt's basement, you're not trying. I walk through the forest of junk back to the laboratory, as Witt calls his room, but the light is out and Witt is not asleep on his bunk. I call his name into the corners for a moment. No answer. There is a chance, I think as I go out into the backyard, that Budd may have really hurt him this time.

Witt is not in the back-lot jungle either. Atom, his German shepherd, is sleeping in a hole, the WITT on his side perfectly legible. He looks like a dead rug. I find all of Witt's bottle-cap men in the back ditch, arranged as they were three days ago when we had a dirt-clod war.

After searching everywhere, even checking in Budd's treasure, the wheelless sea-green Hudson on cinder blocks in the driveway, I sit in the weeds to wait. They give off the wet, dusty smell of late June, nearly choking me. I'll have to tell Witt about this; we could do an experiment. Cool air rises from the geothermal pit, our abandoned attempt to dig to the earth's sixteen-thousand-degree mantle. We quit when the bottom of the funnel-shaped hole consistently read five degrees cooler than the surface.

Rafferty comes into the backyard, his bat over his shoulder. I see him fall in a hole. He stays down a long time and then climbs back up, leaning on his bat. The blind slugger. He told me he stopped wearing his glasses because they were draining his strength. "They give you glasses," he said, "and your eyes get worse and worse. The only way to stop it is to yank them off and give your eyes a workout. The eye is a muscle." Rafferty is so skinny his elbows seem like knots in a new rope. He can bend his arm back at the elbows farther than anyone I've ever seen. Witt did some measurements on them to work on Rafferty's hitting leverage, but nothing came of it. Rafferty can't hit the ball, but he has an amazing swing, which he practices a thousand times a day. He'll suddenly stand up anywhere and start swinging that bat; it's made him a hazard.

I watch Rafferty run the water and drink from the hose. Then, nonchalantly, he turns the hose on Atom, who is still in the hole. I guess he's watching to see if Atom is going to drown in his sleep. The water runs and runs. The hole must be full, but I can't see from here.

I rise from the weeds, leaving an indentation, and walk over to Rafferty. He doesn't see me until I punch his shoulder, then he turns the hose almost on me for a good flashing second. He says, "Witt?"

"Do I look like Witt?"

"Everybody looks like Witt to me."

"It's me, Larry. Everybody looks like me, too, don't they?"

"Hi, Larry. Look at that. Look at this dog." I look

down. Atom is gone except for his head. His eyes and his black nose stick out of the muddy water.

"This dog," Rafferty says, running the water on Atom's face, "has a problem. Hey, I've got something for you." He reaches down with his free hand and works an object out of his back pocket. It takes about two minutes, as he dances and twists until an edge appears, and then a can of mandarin oranges pops out. He hands it to me. "Here. We're all even. Tell Witt to write it in the book."

I take my prize, the beautiful can of tiny oranges, and set it on the ruined washing machine by the fence; then I think better and ditch it in the old fridge way back in the weeds. Returning to Rafferty, I notice a light in the basement window. I go over and see Witt at the lab table looking into Mayreen's violin case. He must have been down there all along.

There hasn't been a violin in that case since January or February, an icy day when Budd pried the instrument from under Mayreen's chin as she sawed through "Three Blind Mice" yet again, and stamped outside onto the driveway where Rafferty, Witt, and I were playing Step Ball in the gray afternoon. Indifferent to us, his face reflecting a pain I hope I never know, Budd looked at the pretty violin the way a man looks at a lit bomb in his

hand, and then he whirled and threw it in a spinning tra-
jectory into the poplars that line the back alley. It hung,
throttled and sprung, in the top of the tallest tree, visible
for ten blocks. Budd exhaled his angry breath the way a
man tears an ugly picture out of a book and went back in
the house, and we marched out to the alley and looked up
at the tragedy.

"I don't want that up there," Witt said. I knew what
he meant. There was stuff in trees and on roofs all
through the neighborhood, signals of mayhem. There
was a bra in a tree down by the river, and bicycle tires
were everywhere. In the winter, with the leaves down,
this stuff glared at us like warnings.

"It's way up," Rafferty said. "You'd fall four times
from up there. Only Roto would climb that high."

We could hear Mayreen wailing from the house. Her
dream was to go on Eugene Jelesnik's talent show, which
was on channel five on Sunday afternoons, and now that
dream was in two wicked pieces above us.

"Did she only know the one song?" Rafferty said.

Witt was wrecked. He would not resume playing Step
Ball, so we sat in the old Hudson for a while. It smelled
of grease and dust and some kind of cherry freshener.
Over the years, we'd driven thousands of miles in that car,

no wheels, no real engine. It had a glass suicide knob affixed to the big steering wheel, and I remember Raff, when he was little, hauling it all the way left, all the way right, as we listened to the wheel hubs grind the cinder-block platform.

What came out of that strategy session was the cross-bow incident, the closest we've come to involving the police in our activities. Witt designed and built a cross-bow, which turned out to be of a larger caliber than we could handle. We bolted a four-by-four onto a seven-foot willow sapling, which was the bow. When we tested it by firing a broom handle off the nylon rope-string, it pene-trated the front of the old washing machine. That was the cool part; the rest was trouble.

Witt was determined to get that violin out of the tree with the crossbow. We practiced with several arrows. We tried some bamboo from the old fort and various pieces of lumber, everything winging away savagely into the trees. Finally Witt pulled an old rake out of the basement. "You guys got a rake?" Rafferty said. He was right: it had never been used. The label was still on the handle.

"I like this," Witt said. "These teeth will catch that violin."

Almost. The rake missed by four feet and disappeared. Witt was grinning because the crossbow worked so well. "With this thing, we could shoot a proper arrow clear to the river," he said.

Rafferty had gone over a block to see where our missiles had landed, and suddenly he came wheeling around the corner waving his arms. "Run!" he called. "Hide." His ears were bright in the cold, and he was pumping steam. "There's a cop!" We piled into the old Hudson and shut the door quietly. Witt went out again and grabbed the crossbow and slid it under the car. Through the smeared and dirty windshield we watched in the brilliant winter sunlight.

Witt was still excited. "I'm telling you," he said. "We can get it. I need one more shot. We need to get another rake." Right then a policeman came around the corner of the alley and looked up and down. He had the rake in his hand. He could walk over here and catch us all in the front seat of this death trap, and it would be on our permanent record. Hiding, a few feet from more trouble than I'd seen so far, I realized the things my mother and father had been telling me about behavior and selecting friends were utterly, blatantly true. I could feel my stomach, sick suddenly and rippling with tribulation.

Then Witt said, "He's gone," and we climbed out of

the musty car, and the air and the day revived me, and Rafferty grabbed my coat and said, "You're going to jail, sonny boy," and we laughed and my stomach straightened right out. We were boys again. Witt looked up at the broken violin and grimaced and shook his head. "My dad's an evil bastard, but did you see that rake fly? Do you think any other kids on any planet whatsoever are doing this stuff?"

Spring came, and the leafy trees hid their terrible secrets. But we all know, even now in this thick, blooming June, that the mangled violin still hangs in the greenery above us all, bad news.

Just the violin case seems bad news. I stand looking in the basement window, and I'm sorry to be seeing it again. Rafferty is now on his hands and knees in the dirt, staring into Atom's canine eyes. The rest of the dog is underwater. "This dog is a crocodile," he says.

"Come on, Rafferty. Witt is in the lab." I pull him up.

"He is?" Rafferty picks up his bat and follows me down into the lab, leaving Atom in the water hole. The dog's eyes follow us. I wonder why Rafferty isn't afraid of going into the basement. He always gets hurt down there. "I've always thought that dog looked like a lizard," he's saying.

Witt is in the lab, unrolling a gnarled extension cord that is heavily taped in three or four places. "Come on," he says. I follow him, and we turn and bump into Rafferty, who is squinting his way along, and we bumble back into the dark junk space.

"Lift that." Witt points to the other side of an old Admiral television cabinet. It's heavy as a safe, and we brutalize it into the other room.

"What," I say, "what? Do you have a new violin?" Just seeing the dark-grained case again cautions me; it's been used for some pretty weird stuff in the last few months.

Witt's face is checkered red and white from trying to lift the heavy television. But he looks different another way, too, as if his eyes have both moved slightly in his face, and his mouth is stapled shut.

"You taking violin lessons?" Rafferty asks. "Gonna go on Eugene Jelesnik's show?"

"Help us, Rafferty." Witt wants to lift the entire television onto the old bureau lab table. I know we'll drop it and be crushed, but after a terrifying minute, somehow it sits right and centers.

"That your machine gun?" Rafferty won't quit about the violin case. Then he finds a *Superboy* comic and scans it closely, his nose right against the pages, reading. It makes sense: blind boy reads in the dark.

"Look," Witt says to me, his eyes still strange, intense.

I lean over the operating table, which is stained with the multiple residues of our many experiments. Witt unclasps the three brass fasteners on the violin case. On the purple velvet inside is what looks like the white belly of a carp, but Witt turns it over, and I see it is Ferguson, his alligator, dead.

"How did he die?"

"Murder. He was murdered by my father."

"Who?" Rafferty says.

"Ferguson."

"Ferguson!" Rafferty jumps up and puts his head in the case. Since he gave up his glasses, he puts his head in things.

"My goddamned father murdered him yesterday. Came home . . ." Witt stops, his throat funny. "Came home, took him out of the tub. Threw him. Out in the Hudson. To bake the shit out of him." I can barely hear Witt's last words, he's run them so low and fast. "This is murder!" he yells, kicking an old shovel.

I remember the warnings. Budd liked to come home from selling paper and take a bath, and he had warned

Witt to keep Ferguson out of the bathtub. I was there one day last year when he came screaming to the back door in a towel. "I'm working for a living!" Budd cried. "I drive all over from dawn till dark, humping my samples up and down stairs, showing people paper, and when I come home, I want to get in my bathtub without any slimy reptiles sleeping in the slimy water!" If you didn't know Ferguson, and didn't see Budd jumping like a lunatic in his towel, his complaint almost made sense.

Now Rafferty sits back with his comic. "Don't tell me," he says. "It's new pet time around here. Right? I recommend a bird. Some kind of really large bird; what about a cormorant? They are huge. Of course, you've always got Atom, the crocodiledog."

Witt drops his arms. "I've got Ferguson," Witt says. I can tell by his voice that we're in for some kind of whole show. "I've had Ferguson for five years, and I still have him."

"Hey, great," Rafferty says. "Great. And I hope you can keep him five more. So that means that it is not new pet time; it's taxidermy experiments, eh, Witt? Am I right?"

Witt takes a running jump and lands both feet in Rafferty's chest, and they go over the old couch into the bicycle stockpile. They are really fighting, and somebody is going to get hurt. It's a pretty good place to fight because all the junk muffles the sound, and there is a lot of stuff with which to hit the other guy. They are mainly crawling over each other slugging, but I can see, from time to time, a flowerpot swung in the half-light, part of a clarinet, the muffled crash of an old iron.

I don't understand fighting and have never fought, really, but these guys go at it once a month, and then they sit up the next minute and are friends. I've considered it and know that it would be more than I could do.

Finally Witt pushes hard and disentangles himself from Rafferty's slug-wrestle. Neither is crying. I know that Rafferty cannot see Witt in the dark cellar, and so I say, "Don't hit me, Rafferty. I'm over here." Witt is quiet against the fruit shelves, trying to still and cover his wheezing breath. He is holding a set of bicycle handlebars, and with two steps he could clock Rafferty into space.

"Don't do it, Witt," I say. "Let it go. Let's do something else. Let's go out and play some Car Baseball." No one says anything. "Besides," I lie, "I think I heard your father come home."

That stops him, and Witt crouches, listening to the

ceiling. We hear a few creaks, his brother Roto up there picking on Mayreen probably, but the mood is broken, and Witt sets the handlebars on the floor. I grab Rafferty, who jumps and wheels his arms when I touch him, but he sits back down and I hand him his comic. He throws it on the floor. "Shit!" he says. "Things are getting strange around here."

"Say you're sorry," I tell Witt. The first time I had to play this role, it was thin ice. Now I know they'll listen.

He comes over, trying to piece his shirt back together. There are no more buttons.

"Say it."

He takes the shirt off and throws it up so it lodges in the pipes, and he puts on his old brown corduroy robe, his lab coat.

"Sorry, Rafferty," he says, looking down to cinch the sash.

"Yeah, oh, yeah. Sorry. Sorry. Things are strange." Rafferty says to me, "Crazy. The goddamned alligator." He points. "That goddamned violin case anyway! Beat up Budd!" Rafferty says. "Punch out your goddamned father. He killed the little bastard. I liked Ferguson." Everybody in this neighborhood knows Ferguson; he's been to school every year for five years, the only alligator anybody has ever seen.

Witt lifts the open violin case like a tray, and Ferguson's belly flashes up at us, the only white thing in this basement world.

"He's dead, Witt," I say, watching my friend. "It's okay. He's dead."

"Yeah, maybe."

Then I sit down by Rafferty, because Witt is thinking it all through, whatever it is going to be. We usually sit in the old Hudson to think, pretend to drive somewhere, bounce in the seats, but now that it killed Ferguson, I can tell those days are over. Rafferty is wincing now at the small print on the advertisement page in *Superboy*. I know what he wants: X-ray Glasses with which he could see through his hand. Rafferty is trying to figure a way the X-ray Glasses would help him become a great hitter, so he could make the Little League all-stars.

Witt is starting to shuffle some of the gear. The towering television cabinet mounted on the table looks like an altar or a rocket, so I figure we're going to have some kind of ritual, but Witt isn't talking.

"I gotta go to baseball practice," Rafferty says, folding the comic into his back pocket and picking up his baseball bat.

"Yeah," Witt says. He lets Rafferty feel his way almost up the stairs before he adds, "You coming back tonight?"

Rafferty turns. "Should I?"

"If you want to." It's enough of a truce, and Rafferty leaves. For a while then, I watch Witt string wires in the back of the old television set. I think he's making a bomb to blow his house out of the ground once his father really does come home. I've never seen him quite this wound up.

"I've gotta go, Witt. I should eat dinner and check in."

"Yeah, sure," he says, dropping his pliers to the floor. "I'll go with you. I should see Rafferty at the park."

So Witt and I ride double through the startling daylight to the park. Linda Aikens and Karen Wilkes are playing tennis, and the swings are alive with kids, one of them my brother, which means my mother hasn't called us yet for dinner. I still have time to get home. It's hard to believe that the neighborhood seethes like this all day long while we're in that basement. Rafferty's team is having batting practice, and we see him leaning on the fence, posing like a professional baseball player, waiting for his turn to bat. Witt watches the pitcher for a while and then goes to Rafferty and says, "Wake up, Bozo."

"Hey, Witt, what are you doing here?"

"Time your step and your swing with this kid's arm. Watch his arm. Keep your back elbow way up and your hands level. Stand up in the box. Don't swing too hard."

"Rafferty," I add, "I think you ought to just wear your glasses." The truth is, I know the real reason he took them off. I was at his house about four weeks ago, the last time he wore them. When his mother's boyfriend Rudy said, "Hey, Four Eyes, get me a beer," his mother laughed, but I don't think it was at Raff. I think she just laughed out of some kind of nervousness or something. She's a nice woman, and beautiful. But I never saw him with those spectacles again.

Rafferty is stepping into the batter's box as I climb onto my bike to leave. "Come back to my house later tonight," Witt says to me. He sees my face and says, "Come on. I'll need some help." I turn to see Rafferty step and swing his beautiful swing and catch nothing but air. He had the timing right, but he was way under it.

At dinner, my father wants to know why I don't spend more time around our house. "What do you guys do all day at the Dimmicks'?"

"Goof around. Play ball."

"Dig holes in the yard," my little brother Eddie adds.

"They let you dig in the yard?"

I've got both hands around a tumbler full of red Kool-Aid, hiding behind it, and I hear myself say, "A little. A few holes."

My father looks out the window at our neighborhood. I try to imagine him jumping up and down with a towel, screaming about an alligator. As a quick conciliation, I ask, "Can those guys sleep out down here tonight?" My mother says yes, but my father, I can tell, is only half glad. It doesn't seem to be why he provided this house, so I could sleep outside of it.

So I go on a bit and say I do spend a lot of time around our house, which is true: I sleep here in a basement room made to light and order by my father's own hands; I occasionally play or sleep out in our backyard, which is squared by the mower every Friday, no weed in sight. I love to return to my own home, this haven, after being torn and spun upside down by the world.

My father has the only working lawn mower in the neighborhood. It has a little two-stroke Briggs and Stratton engine that purrs like a sewing machine. Every Friday afternoon when he comes home from his welding job at Glendale Bridge and Iron Company, he checks the oil and starts the lawn mower, still in his work khakis, and he mows our lawn. It is, in many ways, the only lawn in the neighborhood. Little kids, Raff's brother Markie and Witt's brother Roto and others, gather at the edges of our property to watch my father march in concentric squares and to smell the wonderful cut grass. After he finishes, they will sneak in barefoot and feel the lush cut surface.

How can I tell my mother and father that Witt is dangerous in a way I do not understand; that he hates and would like to kill his father; that he even calls his father by his first name; and that, in a basement overgrown with foul junk, we are trying to discover the laws that make the world work. It is all a special chaos.

My father sighs. He is about to make the leap from a few holes in Witt's backyard to Willie Bynum. The first thing that happened this spring was that a kid named Willie Bynum got killed. Bynum was three years older than we were; he'd pitched for the Red Hats when we were rookies. He and Parley and Bynum's uncle had been out hunting rabbits at the old Camp Harmony firing range. Willie Bynum had found a small artillery shell about the size of a flashlight, and when he picked it up it exploded, and the base of the thing went through his head, and parts got in his uncle's arm and one piece went through Parley's ear.

From time to time there were accidents like this on the old firing range, but somehow Willie Bynum, whom we'd kind of known, who'd been a tough pitcher, believe me, when he dies, my parents are all over me double. Be careful and stay away from the river! It's filthy and will tangle and drown you for sure, and drowning is awful. And stay away from the railroad tracks, the train will suck you under its steel wheels and your foot will get caught in the trestle. And why are you hanging out with Witt again digging holes and doing God knows what?

I come home once a week skinned up or smelling bad or with my shirt burned or with puke on one sleeve, and they want to know, can't I play with other kids? They don't see Ivan Kidder or Tim Torkelson at the center of any messes, they say. I want to answer: that's because Kidder and Torkelson are almost thirteen and chasing the girls. They're one year out of Little League and running around this summer in their school clothes, retired fat cats.

I mention that I also hang out a lot with Rafferty, and my mother sighs and says, "His mother isn't married," which I don't understand at all. Mrs. Rafferty, whose first name is Terri Ann, has her boyfriend, Rudy the Rude, who rides a fenderless motorcycle and wears a Levi's jacket with his name in ball-point ink across the back six inches high. Sometimes I look at my parents and I try to imagine my father in a Levi's jacket with his name on the back: STANLEY. STAN. BIG STAN THE MAN. It won't go. I'd like to ask Witt about this, but I know what he would say: Human behavior. Trouble. Stay out.

"If you find a bullet or an unexploded shell," my mother says now, jumping in, "don't touch it! Don't pick it up! Just move away from it and come home and tell your father where it is."

My father nods at me grimly and says, "Move away, Larry. Don't pick it up." I look at them both, the worry stark on their faces, and I agree with them heartily, nodding, and saying I won't, I would never pick it up. But in my heart, I know I am the kind of kid who, when he sees something glittering on the ground, is going to reach for it.

Finally I say to my father, "I'm not going to touch anything dangerous. I'm being careful. But can I go down to the Dimmicks' for a while? Witt's pet alligator died. He's pretty upset." My parents look at each other. These poor people; I'm being hard on them.

"Ferguson?" my brother Eddie says. "Ferguson died?"

＊　＊　＊

Riding my bicycle down the two blocks to Witt's
house at twilight, I nearly sing with happiness and free-
dom. I swerve down the broad-humped street, waving at
families on porches. The trees, heavy with June's leaves,
rise and bend above me. At the end of this tunnel of trees,
the sunset shows three tiers of brown, yellow, and purple.
I love my life, though I couldn't explain it to anybody. I
approach Witt's junk pile of a yard, pumping faster,
teething wind, and as I lower a shoulder and swerve
between the old Hudson and the cracked back step, my
eyes water against the fast air and I think: no one knows
me, my heart; it is different than anyone knows.

Rafferty is helping Witt by the time I arrive. In the
light of the desk lamp and one portable clamp bulb, they
have stretched wires in a spiderweb across the basement,
each hooking into the old Admiral television set. Witt has
spliced his old model train transformer into the wiring
between the dials on the TV. He sends me out back to get
a wash pan full of water.

As I step cautiously back down the stairs, I ask, "Okay,
Witt. What is it now? What are we making . . . dinner?"

"We're going to save him."

"Who, Rafferty?"

"Ferguson."

"Ferguson," I say, stopping on the bottom step, "is dead."

"Then we're going to revive him."

"You can't do that." I'm standing still.

"You're spilling the water," Rafferty notes.

"Yeah. We can do it. I've thought it over."

"He's *dead*, Witt."

"Dead? Dead?" Witt says, taking the water and setting the pan inside the back of the television set. "Do you know what *dead* is? Do you? Who told you what dead is? I'd like to know."

"What about Willie Bynum?" I say. "He's dead."

"Yes he is." Witt points a finger at my face and then waves it. "But he blew himself up. His head was damaged and there was no . . ."

"Repairing it?" Rafferty says.

"Right. Parley said the hole was that big." Witt makes a fist. "A guy is not going to work at all after something like that."

"He was a good pitcher," Raff says. "That high overhand stuff. Did he have a curve?"

"Wicked," I say. "It dropped off the table real hard."

"He's dead," Witt says.

"What about Jerry Sallis?" Rafferty says from where he's sitting on a wooden barrel, watching our argument. "No one revived him. Remember last summer? He drowned at Echo Reservoir. I saw him at the funeral, dead. No one revived him. At all."

Witt doesn't answer, lifting Ferguson out of the violin case and slipping him right side up into the pan of water. "Well," he says, "they should have. It's all hearsay; that's all we're getting. I know nothing about being dead." He shakes his head. "Ferguson's waiting. You guys want to try this, or forget it?"

It takes us about an hour to tape the wires to Ferguson. Witt put him in the water too soon and he got slimy, and we had to take him out and dry him off, poor little guy. Then I held him while Witt ran three loops of paper masking tape around. Six separate wires.

Witt places Ferguson back into the metal pan and then sprinkles a green powder into the water. "We're all set," he says.

Rafferty creeps upstairs and outside, and we hand him the transformer through the broken basement window. I climb the stairs and watch Witt circle the entire mechanism, adjusting the three knobs in front of the set and then plugging it in. In the focused light, wearing one blue Playtex Living Glove, no shirt under that brown robe, and thirty cowlicks along the little scar on his head from the cat incident, Witt looks flat-out deranged. I love it. He lifts both hands slightly as if to hold the applause and skips up the steps behind me. We are all set.

The backyard is a rage of crickets as always, and Rafferty is groaning at something, which turns out to be Atom trying to hump his leg. Rafferty tries to fend Atom off, and the dog starts mouthing Rafferty's whole arm, and soon they are on the ground.

"Don't pick on the dog, will ya, Rafferty?" Witt says.

But Rafferty is lost, at least until he remembers to roll in a ball and play dead. Atom stands and shakes, chagrined, then strolls away and lounges in one of the holes in the yard. Atom never attacks me; it must be something about the way skinny people like Rafferty smell.

"You ready?" Witt whispers to me when we are lying on the ground, peering in the window.

"Let's go."

Now Witt has the transformer, and I can hear the lever nicking over the raised dashes on the dial, and then Witt snaps it full right. Inside the basement, a buzz emerges, steady, weird, and even, like a dial tone. I inch back from the window. Rafferty is leaning over our shoulders, saying, "Hear that?" There is a series of blitzing blue flashes, ten, twelve, arcing inside off the walls, and the smell of electricity gone wrong as the buzz begins to rise, sirenlike, into a razor wail that keens right out of ear range, and Atom begins a ravaged-gut-deep howl behind us. I've never heard him howl before. The television tube goes white, filling with electric milk, swelling, or so it seems.

Witt takes my arm and says, "Watch out!" But the tube explodes as he speaks, and the night becomes a fifty-gallon drum being kicked and kicked. I reach for the house, but it is gone. Then I see I am ten feet back from the window. Atom is whining in his foxhole. Rafferty comes from somewhere behind me and grabs my arm, lifting me up, and says, "Did you hear that?" There are weeds in his collar. My ears are full of a sweet, humming static, and my eyes float with sparking black commas. A thin, gaseous kind of smoke is trailing out the window, where Witt still lies, angling this way and that on the ground, trying to get a better look. He pushes himself up. "Come on," he says. "We have to go inside."

On the back porch, Witt stops us to tie on cloth face

masks. He takes my head in both hands and tilts it to the porch light.

"Look at that."

Rafferty comes over and looks at my head. I reach up into my hair and feel the wetness. "Hold still," Witt says, tightening his grip and plucking a tiny section of hair right out of my head. He lets go and holds a bright glass sliver in front of my face. "You've been stabbed."

"Have I got one?" Rafferty says, bending down to show his scalp.

"Yours went clear through." Witt passes him and enters through the smoke.

"That's not really funny, Witt," Rafferty says, putting a hand on my shoulder to follow me into the basement.

Downstairs, there is nothing to see. The wispy, sour, iridescent smoke lingers everywhere, pooling thickest against the ceiling, and Witt cannot make the lights work. We feel our way around until Rafferty says, "Here it is, over here." Being blind, he's an ace in the dark. We join him at the television; it's still hot.

Witt crawls around behind and strikes a match in the interior of the set. The flash reveals little: the cabinet is bombed out and fried; everything is black. Another match and Witt says, "He's gone! Ferguson's gone!"

"But not forgotten," Rafferty says. "Now let's get some air and hit the pharmacy for a root beer before it closes."

"Listen!" Witt hisses, and we stand scared still.

"What?"

"Just listen." And there is a scampering behind me toward the furnace room. "It's him!" Witt cries. "Ferguson!" There is more scampering against the lumber pile and past the fruit jars. "That's him, Rafferty! That is Ferguson!" But Rafferty is gone, scared up the stairs.

"You think it is, Witt?"

"Oh, *yeah*!" He is triumphant. "That's him. I'll show you; come here." I move back to the former television set. There is more noise behind us on the floor, and Witt laughs aloud. "Now look." We look again into the old, cooked TV, and Witt scratches a match. In the flare, I see the wash pan Ferguson was wired into. "See this." Witt points to a tiny claw mark in soot on the side of the dish. It is as if something had crawled out. "I'm sorry about old Willie Bynum; he could really throw the ball, but this is what we know about death, right here! And that is all we know except for our guy Ferguson living it up behind us." His match burns out, but Witt finishes:

"All that we know about being dead. The rest is a bunch of radically ignorant hearsay!"

Outside again, Witt asks, "How's your head?"

"Fine. I'm fine." I feel the place and it's swollen and sore, but fine. I like that it's in my hair; my mother won't see it.

"Good. We've got one more thing." He clips his sleeping bag onto my bike, and we lay the bicycles in the weeds by the alley, out of sight. Witt is so happy that every once in a while he mutters, "Old Ferguson," and pushes Rafferty into one of the holes. But when Rafferty joins us by the Hudson, Witt says, "Here, Bozo, you get the honors; you fought for them." Witt drags a tire iron from under the front end, and he taps a hole in the windshield and hands Rafferty the tool. "Ventilate each window," he whispers. "This particular Hudson will bake no more alligators."

Rafferty moves around the car, his head up close, tapping the windows one at a time. For a guy who can't see, he does a neat job. Then Witt comes running from somewhere behind me, and in three steps he is standing on the roof of the old car pouring gasoline through all the newly opened spaces. He only has a little in a jelly jar. Finally he drops the glass container through the windshield and then jumps to the ground beside me.

Witt grins. "Any questions?" Witt shows us his matches.

"He loves that car."

"He does love that car." Witt nods, grinning.

"We're going to get in trouble for this one."

"Yep," Witt says definitely. "At least I am. But old Budd is in trouble now. With me. I'll tell you something about human behavior. Sometimes you can be so mad you can taste it." He swallows and smiles. "I can taste it now. Budd can come home and put out a fire and *then* it will be my turn. Then Ferguson can grow up, secretly, bigger than Atom, and bite my father's head off some night and I'll be free." He laughs and adds, "These things are, of course, in the future."

We slip back and hide in the weeds, their acrid smell like danger, and Raff says, "Budd's going to kill you for this."

"Kill me?" Witt laughs; his eyes vanish and he rocks back and forth happily. He takes my shoulder for balance, and I see he is still laughing silently. "He may just kill me."

That's how this crushing summer starts. We're waiting in the thick alfalfa musk of the giant alley weeds on the deepest night I have known so far, waiting for Witt's father to come home from selling paper all day long so we can light the Hudson into orange fire and race down the alley alive. Plunging through dark places at that speed will be like flying.

3 the speed of light

Theoretical mathematics comes closest to describing the speed of light, but the fieldwork has made a contribution. Early efforts observing the moons of Jupiter and later experiments with rotating mirrors and reflectors were surprisingly accurate in their measurement of the velocity at which waves of light traveled.

It's funny how we pick up and just go about our business over the next few days: Little League practice, sodas at the pharmacy, roaming on our bicycles from project to project. Witt won't talk about what happened after the car fire. We did burn up the Hudson a little, a tiny blaze that barely had a toehold when Budd threw a gallon of milk on it. He was moving pretty fast, and we fled. In his agitation, Budd has been tough on everybody. Witt got cuffed for it, I think, but wouldn't go into it. One of his ears turned blue. Slightly charred and smelling like burned custard, the defeated car simply settled deeper into the driveway.

Our new projects tend to be in the physical sciences, mostly because of what happened a month ago, before school was even out, when Witt's curiosity almost killed his cat. He wanted to see what a cat was, and his best bet, he figured, was to shave Lazy, their yellow tabby. Rafferty got the cat to sleep on his lap and then Witt tenderly massaged Budd's shave cream into her fur. We all leaned in, amazed that she was so purple under that yellow coat. It took a long time for him to hack down through the thick fur and get to the skin, and the cat hair and Barbasol fumes were at me pretty good, so I went up into the backyard to sit in the weeds and breathe real air.

Roto and Mayreen, Witt's younger brother and sister, were chasing Atom around the yard. Some days the dog was persecuted. The WITT on his side in gray letters looked like an advertisement of some kind. Atom himself was a huge German shepherd with a hip problem, so that his run was more of a sidle, and he slid around the yard like two little guys in a bad dog suit.

It was then I heard a scream that shook the house,

and I saw a flaming blur, golden and purple, shoot through the broken panes of the basement window. It was Lazy. Witt had snarled Budd's safety razor in her matted hair, and she had come to, bare naked on one side, and, using Witt's scalp as a runway, had taken flight. Atom caught a whiff of the sweet shave cream and went off after her, nose down like a stock car. The dog came back later that night, but we were sure that cat was gone forever. "Cats, dogs, the animal kingdom," Witt says. "Too many variables."

Now, since Lazy's departure (and his own stitches) and the hard night with Ferguson, Witt wants to study only the physical sciences. So we spend a day making a waterwheel out of an old bike rim we found on top of Smalls' sheds. We wire some empty soup cans to the edge and stick it in the riverbank on a four-foot piece of steel rebar. It struggles around and around, moaning with each revolution.

"This is a genuine hydroelectric breakthrough," Rafferty says. He's begun massaging his eyes with his fists all the time, convinced the increased circulation will improve his vision. "Remember that film in Compton's class on Boulder Dam? Will this deal make electricity?"

"We're going to measure how fast the river is going," Witt says. He's already got his notebook out.

"What are we trying to prove?" Rafferty says.

"We don't know that!" Witt says. "If we knew that, we wouldn't get to do all this stuff. You want a worksheet like Durrant's class had so you can fill in the blanks?"

Rafferty says, "I wouldn't mind." He rolls his eyes, his whole head, his entire body, but Witt grabs the sleeve of his T-shirt.

"Listen. We're looking around, that's all. If you take what you're given, you're asking to be crushed by what you don't even know! We need to find some things out. If we don't, we'll end up like Budd, pissed off and ticking. You want to be a guy who throws everything he can't understand, hits stuff, pounds on people?" Witt is right up in Rafferty's face, and Raff jerks away and walks down the bank.

"You pound Mayreen," he says.

"See!" Witt calls to the sky, his arms open. "See! We've got to keep busy!"

In the murky eddy of the river at his feet, something suddenly appears, a dull white flash. It's the belly of a carp, and Witt kneels in a second and flips the fish onto the bank.

"Bring him along," he tells me.

"What is it?" Rafferty says. "What are we going to do?"

"Autopsy."

In the basement, the burned Admiral television cabinet still stands on top of the bureau, which is Witt's lab table. "Take that outside," he tells us. "Put it out by the fridge." The set is heavy as a safe, but the idea of throwing it into the weeds powers us up the stairs and out the back. While we're struggling with it, I see Witt strap on his goggles and snap on that one blue rubber glove.

When we return, Witt has the carp on the bureau and has ripped it open with a pair of old scissors.

"I thought we weren't doing any more animal kingdom stuff," says Raff.

"We aren't." Witt holds up the fish and looks into it like a person searching for keys in a purse.

"That fish is in the animal kingdom," Rafferty goes on.

"This fish is dead. He isn't in any kingdom."

"God's kingdom?"

"You're in God's kingdom, Rafferty." Witt hovers over his work, not looking up. "You're the only one in this room in God's kingdom. The rest of us are scientists." He nips the little stomach open with his pocketknife and presses the gray pouch with his thumb; a pulp of refolded waterbugs and weeds pops out.

"What'd he die of, Witt?" Rafferty says.

Witt ignores him, saying slowly, "We come from fish, you know."

"I came from Grand Junction," Rafferty says.

While Witt searches for the heart amid the gnarled little mass of tubular wetnesses, I step away and let Rafferty have a better look. From the stairs that lead to fresh air, I turn and see my two friends leaning into the light as if gambling. I hear Rafferty say, "What'd he eat? Did that stuff kill him, Witt?"

During the fish operation, I've been listening to Witt's mother's footsteps as she moves around upstairs. Mrs. Dimmick is the most tolerant parent in history, enduring the mess and the noise, the smoke and the smell, Budd and his regular tirades and persecutions, the general house abuse and minor damage that Witt engenders all around her. There are times when something will fall and crash in the basement, the kind of stunning racket that would stop my house for two days at least and change four of the major rules, but a moment later we can hear Witt's mother humming or putting cups away. If she uncovers one of the mason jars containing our water samples or forgotten experiments, a smell mushrooms forth and forces her from her own home. At odd times she suddenly appears in the yard, hanging onto the clothesline, coughing until all the laundry falls to the ground.

That night, with the results of the autopsy still clotting on top of the basement bureau, Lazy returns. We are all sleeping out in Witt's backyard in a weedy campsite, still trying for the old sleep-out record set by Parley two years before: ninety-nine times in a row. Our lives are a series of record attempts, and I've learned from Witt the double pleasure of doing something and then writing it down.

The cat comes back for the fish. I see something, a figure emerging from the ruined basement window; it's the carp floating out the charred frame, but then I see that it's riding in Lazy's mouth. The familiar yellow specter, one side shaved clean, scampers right across our sleeping bags and into the alley. The cat has the fish, most of it. Our experiments are eating each other.

A second later here comes Atom, clambering through the window like an ape being born, clawing up, snapping the last crosspiece. He whips by in a low slide, flinging wood slivers upon us and slipping under the fence. Even with that hip he can move when he has to.

"That cat is trouble, Witt," Rafferty says. "She's off kilter with that haircut."

"Oh, you're crazy." Witt stands and walks over to admire the new hole in his basement. "That cat is fully recovered. Her appetite has come back."

We pick debris off our sleeping bags for a while and get in them, and then the lights inside Witt's house go out and the neighborhood grows real quiet.

"We come from fish, you know," Rafferty says to Witt.

"Eight," Witt says. "Ninety-two more and we've got the record." We'll have to sleep out until early October to have a shot. Witt lies back, his eyes full of the night sky. "Stars," he says.

"Where?" Rafferty says. He struggles out of his sleeping bag and stands up, hoisting his bat. He assumes his stance, and we hear the perfect *swish, swish, swish* of his beautiful swing for a while. He cuts a black silhouette out of the jillion scattered stars that flare and sizzle in rattling clusters.

"Are we looking up or down?" I ask Witt. I can see some red stars, some blue.

Witt is quiet and then he whispers it: "The speed of light."

In the morning, the sun bakes us out with its hot hammer, and we throw our sleeping bags on the fence and hit the pharmacy for a sugar breakfast of frosted root beers and red licorice. Then it's scouring the park for lost tennis balls, playing Drifter, the game where you see who can go the farthest on our bikes without pedaling. That leads us down to the river and throwing rocks at flotsam, and by noon, we're clear across the railroad tracks trying to talk Rafferty into putting his belt buckle on the tracks. The train is coming.

He finally relents, and we hide in the willows as the freight train pounds slowly by, forty-seven cars. As it passes, I note that I'm holding on to one of the little trees.

"Can you get sucked under the train?" I ask Witt.

Rafferty has started out after his newly smashed belt buckle when Witt grabs him. He points and we see Parley ride by, sitting on the steps of the caboose deck. He's hitched a lift on his way home from his summer job down at Shumway Lumber. He doesn't see us. Parley rides past the trestle, then stands and swings by one arm off the train. He lands in a smooth four-step stride run and then breaks into his fluid walk, crossing the tracks and heading up Concord.

"Let's follow him," Witt hisses. "Come on!"

"What?" I say. "Why?"

"Come on, Larry," Rafferty says. "This is better than cutting up that fish."

We race down Western Street and cut over into the vacant lot. Parley angles across the end of the street and strides through the park. We follow, all of us keeping our heads low, as if anybody ever noticed us. We ditch our bikes against the old rest room and dance around and through the tennis courts, crossing Derby Street and into the hedge back of the Wilkeses'. From here we have a remarkable view: Old Man Wilkes, who is retired, is outside his back door hosing off his blue Plymouth, and behind his shed Parley has just met up with Karen Wilkes. The gray shed is right between them. There are two bicycle tires and three or four boots on the ruined tar-paper roof. Parley gives something to Karen and puts his arm around her. When the old man calls her name, they push apart and Parley drifts with those long, loping strides down the cinder alley toward the junior high. Karen goes into the shed and then comes out quickly and walks around to her father to help him wipe down the car.

"This is cool," Rafferty says. "This is far superior to dipping muck out of the river."

"Right," I say. "Now let's go play Over the Line."

"Let's not," Witt says. "Just yet." He leads us the long way around to the side of the Wilkeses' shed, and then he actually goes into the dark space. There's a grimy workbench and some furniture: a couch and a coffee table and a couple of old standing lamps in the corner.

"What are we looking for?" Rafferty says. "Another rake?" There's a barrel of lawn tools behind the door.

"This," Witt says, lifting a fat candle off the coffee table.

"We've got ten candles at your house," Rafferty says. "What we need are more matches." Matches have been real tight in the neighborhood in the last few weeks. There was our little fire in Budd's Hudson and somebody burned the tennis courts' nets, and suddenly all the match drawers are empty. We've got one-half book left, which we found in the trash behind Favorite Pharmacy.

"Did Parley give her a candle?" I ask Witt.

"Parley's been here," Witt says. He goes over to the little window and looks out across to the park. "And he's coming back."

"Now?" Rafferty says. "Where is he?" He sidles to the

door and looks out. Witt pushes him outside, and I follow him back to our bikes.

"No, not now," Witt says, mounting his bike. "Tonight."

After Little League practice and dinner, the three of us meet up at Rafferty's, throwing our sleeping bags onto the clay. His backyard has a shiny new chain-link fence guarding this strange dirt terrace. They're going to put in a yard someday, Rafferty says. It's been this barren for an eon. A little carpet of thornos, a flat, lacy weed, grows around the perimeter, but otherwise we could be on the moon. We don't sleep out here three times all summer. There's nothing to hide behind if you have to take a leak.

Rafferty lies on his ratty zipperless sleeping bag and rubs his eyes. He looks kind of like Elvis when the light is right and when he's lying on the ground not looking at you. It's after dinner and we're free with hours of daylight, which might as well be piles of money; this time of day makes me feel rich and ready for the next thing. We tramp down the alley, our shadows twenty feet tall, to the park where Rafferty's little brother Markie is playing in a minor league game.

Markie is eight, and we taught him how to throw a

slow curve this spring, which makes him the best pitcher his age in the entire state. When he can get it over the plate. Usually he walks a few guys and they steal and score on pass balls; the score of all minor league games is 20 to 20.

We fan out and start playing Foul Ball, one point for retrieving each foul that the minor leaguers hit, two points if you field it while it's still moving, and five if you catch a pop foul in the air. Witt has got the aggregate scores going back through last summer. The park is in full swing, and so are my chances for swindling Rafferty.

I've always done it. He's lazy, and he makes it too easy. I buy an orange snow cone from the concession shack and eat half of it noisily, slurping at the bright nectar and generally making a little show out of it. Rafferty, who I know is stone broke, starts to fidget. "Raff," I say.

"Don't do it, Rafferty," Witt says.

"Witt," I tell him. "I'm talking here to my pal Raff." And then I give him the spiel. He can have the rest of my snow cone, the white ice level with the top of the paper cone, only a faint stain of orange left, for, let's see: ten cents *credit*. It cost me ten cents. I wave it once under his nose and he's done for; his hand goes out and takes it, and I say to Witt, "If you'd be so kind as to record our transaction."

Witt turns, disgusted, but he has an overwhelming belief in scrupulous records, and so he leafs through his papers and writes the little numbers in the right square. Last summer, we started our record books, which are really clipboards we made from pieces of old linoleum, and in them we keep the standings and averages for all the various baseball leagues we've got going. In addition, Witt keeps a dozen yellow sheets where he records the money, who owes whom and how much.

This evening there are no foul balls at all, and so we sit on the top row of the third-base bleachers under the giant sycamores and watch the game for a while. Across the way on the first base side sit Mrs. Rafferty and Rudy the Neanderthal. They don't exactly match, this guy in his Levi's vest and the elegant Mrs. Rafferty, who is the most beautiful woman in the neighborhood. She doesn't look like any of the mothers we know. She wears dresses and does not holler at twilight for her kids to come for dinner, the way everyone else in our neighborhood does. Mrs. Rafferty is delicate and calm. She is careful, never hurried, and she always calls me by my full name: Lawrence. I'm smart enough to know

I've got a little crush on her.

She is careful to maintain in a large closet in her base-ment a pantry fully stocked with one year's supply of food—in case of earthquake, famine, or nuclear holo-caust. There are bread and crackers and tuna fish and, among other things, tins of mandarin oranges. Evidently Mrs. Rafferty's plan is to feed her family tuna fish sand-wiches right after the earthquake. Her church advised her to store all of this food, and she is always advising Rafferty to be prudent and provident. These are words he hasn't mastered.

We all know the last part of my evil swindling, in which Rafferty gets utterly even through no sacrifice of his own. In a day or two or three or four, we will be back here in the empty park at midday, stretched out on the bleachers taking sun, and I will say, "Rafferty, you know that dime you owe me? Well, I'd be willing to clear the books for, say, one can of mandarin oranges. Your mother's never going to miss one can."

"Do I owe him a dime?" Rafferty will ask Witt, and Witt will turn to his clipboard and say yes.

"One can." Rafferty will nod, lost in the wonderful logic of being able to keep all of his spending money for our trips to the Favorite Pharmacy soda fountain. So

Rafferty will cruise quickly home and Witt will moan again at me as he crosses out the debt.

I always tell Witt, "Don't complain. I'm doing him a favor. Besides, he'll bring you some crackers."

And soon Rafferty will return and toss me a can of those sweet baby oranges, and Witt and Rafferty will grumble over their crackers. I always open the can from the bottom, using my old Forest Master pocketknife, because the purple fifty-nine cents sticker printed on the top bothers me. A little.

Now, content with his part of the deal, Rafferty sucks on the snow cone until it's nothing but a twisted bit of soggy orange paper, and then he gnaws on that until Witt takes the pathetic mess away from him and throws it to the ground. Meanwhile Rudy the Savage has been cheering heartily for Little Markie, standing up, clapping, pounding the fence, all the stuff some parents do every night. Mrs. Rafferty sits quietly, occasionally clapping. Witt stares at the guy and asks Rafferty, "Where's your real dad?"

"Grand Junction."

"Yeah, well, check this," Witt says, and he arches and tugs two watches from his pocket. They are both his father's old watches, but they have been keeping identical time for two days. Witt repaired them himself. We squint at the second hands.

"Bulova," I say.

"Are they okay?"

"You shouldn't rub your eyes so much, you'd be able to see them," Witt tells Rafferty. "Come on."

We leave the bleachers, weaving down between all the adults, and go around by the snack shack. Witt says he's going to measure the distance between the backstop and the bandstand, which is at the other end of the park, down by Nevada Avenue. He starts counting his steps. "I'll be up there," he says, pointing at the top of the back-stop. "And you guys will be down there." He points to the bandstand roof.

"And why is that?" Rafferty says.

"So we have a clear line of sight for the experiment."

"And the experiment is about falling off the backstop? Keith Gurber already did that last year. Remember? We were here. It sure looked like it hurt."

Witt stops counting on his twenty-fifth step and turns to Raff. "The way we find anything out, Mister, is by observation and measurement." He waves his hand out in a gesture meant to take in the whole world. "We're going to measure the speed of light."

"You're following this," Rafferty says to me. Before I can answer, there is a general whooping, and we turn to see seven or eight mitts fly into the sky. I love the minor leaguers. At the end of every game the team that is on the field squeals with joy and throws their mitts, win or lose. They holler and jump, just happy that the exercise is over. Mrs. Rafferty and Rudy the Armpit are up, his arm around her, and they are shepherding young Markie, and from here they look like a little family. I'm glad Rafferty can't see it.

A few minutes later, in the new dark, we are sitting on the bandstand roof. Witt found out it is 405 paces from the backstop. You crawl up through the rafters and there is a small hole in the roof, and from the top you can see Nevada Avenue and the traffic all the way to the river. Most of the cars have their lights on in the thickening dusk. I can see my house a block away. My parents have no idea that I'm on the bandstand roof, that I've been up here a dozen times. They deserve a better son, but this is science, adventure, life on earth.

"What's that?" Raff asks. There's a form lying on one slope of the roof.

I crawl over there and see it is a blue girl's bike, fenders and white walls. "It's Benny's sister's bike," I say.

"Cling threw it up here," Witt says.

"That's a pretty good throw for a bike."

Witt straps one of the watches onto his wrist and presses the other into my palm. He holds his little Roy Rogers flashlight lit against the face of the watch in my hand. When he pulls it away, the dial on the Bulova prints itself in the dark distinctly.

"Cool," Rafferty says, taking the watch into his hand and putting his finger on the bright watch face. "Is that the speed of light?"

"Raff," Witt says to him. He's almost angry. "You ever look at the sun?"

"Plenty. Every time I play right field."

"Well, that's not the sun you're seeing."

"Yes it is, Witt. I look up for the fly ball and the sun puts my eyes out. It's the sun, Witt, that big, bright thing that is up all day."

I hear Witt sit back and exhale. After a moment, he whispers, "That's not the sun. That's just the light it is sending. The sun has moved on! It takes the light a while to get here!"

"How long, like a week?"

"That's what we are going to find out right now."

"Isn't it in a book?"

"A book!" Witt says. He stands in the dark and goes down to Benny's sister's bike and pushes it off the roof, and we hear the muffled clatter. "This is the world, Rafferty! What do we need a book for?"

"Say you're sorry," I tell Rafferty.

"Oh," he says, "I am sorry. I'm sorry that all I want to do is catch a pop-up and not have my eyes burned out, and I'm sorry that my little brother can throw a better curve than I can, and I'm sorry that I'm up here with you two geniuses when I could be home playing Furniture Tag," he says. He starts climbing down, but Witt catches his shirt and says, "Shhhhhh!" Our three heads are close together, and then we see Parley walk out of the dark and across the lit tennis courts, headed for the Wilkeses'.

"That's us," Witt says. "Come on. Put the watch in your pocket for now."

We help one another down through the roof and then stand in the alley, where it is more dark than light. We can see into all the back windows along the way; everybody's eating dinner, doing dishes, smoking cigarettes in the yellow light. At the Wilkeses', Witt grabs Rafferty's shirt again and we all wait in the hedge, breathing. We can see the lights on in the house and the dark shed.

"We're good," he whispers.

"What can you see?" Rafferty says.

We're all staring into the dark as hard as we can; there's some noise, and then I see a sudden square of light float against the black shed wall, and I realize it is the little window. "What is it?" I ask.

The light washes and wanes faintly, a weird glow. Witt is hunkered down, creeping toward the window. By the time we follow and join him, he's standing on a wheelbarrow, peering in, his eyes just above the sill.

"What do you see?"

"Shhhhhh!"

"Here," Witt says to me, pointing how I should step up on the wheelbarrow.

Inside, the candle blinks and flashes on the cherry table, and I can see the edges of things ripple and disappear, the neat row of glass jars on the workbench full of bolts and screws, a wrench or two. The window is dirty, but something bizarre is happening.

"What is it?" I whisper to Witt.

"That's Karen Wilkes."

Rafferty bumps me from behind, and I grab Witt's shoulder to keep from going down. "Raff! Easy."

The figure on the couch has four arms. I want to rub

the window, clean it, and then I see Karen is lying back against Parley, half on his lap, and his face is working against the side of her face. The light wanders and catches on Karen's teeth, the inside of her knee in her cutoff Levi's, the copper zipper bright and open, and Parley's hand thrust in her shorts. Karen sat ahead of me in social studies, Miss Talbot's class, and wore a yellow dress once a week, which was my favorite. In the strange light now she has her arm up around Parley's neck as they push together.

"Larry," Raff says from behind me, "what's this? What's coming?"

I misunderstand Rafferty until he tugs at my shirt, and I turn to the house and see the outline of Old Man Wilkes through the white light of the open doorway two seconds before we hear the screen door clatter and feel the wheelbarrow buckle and slide, scraping against the shed as we come down. Rafferty still has my shirt, luckily, because when I jump up and dash into the vacant lot, he's right behind me. I run until I feel the ground drop away sickeningly, and I take two steps in air before slugging into the far side of our old dirt fort. I roll before Rafferty can fall on me, but he still gets me in the shoulder with his knee when he comes down. Witt is already at the lip of the old fort, struggling to see what's going on now at the Wilkeses'.

I heard breaking glass while we were racing away and now I hear a door slam twice and then Karen's voice, maybe "No, no!" or "Oh!"

"What'd you guys see in there? What was going on?" says Raff. We wait, leaning in the dirt bank, breathing hard.

"Nothing," Witt says to Rafferty. He is looking at me. "We didn't see anything. An old shed, dark as hell." I've been in this hole a hundred times since I was seven years old. I remember dashing around some afternoon years ago, playing army and pretending to be shot as I ran for safety, sliding in here on my back headfirst and staring at the clouds for twenty minutes, each the size and shape of a different state—California, Ohio, Montana—as I lay dead and listened to the living soldiers calling out and making gun noises with their mouths.

Now there is more commotion, lights in the house going on and off, and then the headlights of Old Man Wilkes's Plymouth flash and sweep the field in which we hide. The engine growls steadily. When we look up again, red beams are flashing in the dusty air like dragon's eyes coming our way, and then they stop and smolder, and in the purple smoke, Mr. Wilkes crosses back and forth dragging what sounds like a chain.

"Run!" Rafferty says. Behind us I can see the park, the empty tennis courts lit like an island of safety. And then the Plymouth's engine hums a deeper tune and louder, and we hear the unmistakable scream of lumber breaking with popping glass, and then there is a noise so loud, a crash that jolts us up out of the old fort and we are running for our lives through the field, down the alley, across Derby Street to the park. Running at night is different from running in the day. It is four times as fast, five times. If I could move like this stealing second, I'd lead the league. We slide into the lush grass behind the home-run fence, the Favorite Pharmacy sign at the right-field foul line.

"Did he kill Parley?" I ask.

"What was that noise?" Rafferty says.

Witt is beached out against the fence. "I think he's pulled his own shed down."

Rafferty pokes his head over the fence as if he could see. "You ever hear of anybody doing that?" he says. "That's a new one."

Witt gets up and starts walking toward Rafferty's house and our sleeping bags. "Wait a minute, Witt. What about the speed of light?" I say. My heart is still thumping.

"What about it?"

I stare him down. "Let's do what we said we'd do."

"Okay. Okay," he says. "Let's measure the speed of light."

With the flashlight, Witt recharges the dial of the watch he gave me, and he goes off in the blackness 405 paces to climb the twenty-foot backstop. Rafferty and I scramble up the rafters and onto the bandstand and sit straddling the roof, watching the headlights on Nevada Avenue, waiting for his signal.

"What did you guys see?" Raff asks.

I hesitate and then say, "It was Parley and Karen Wilkes."

"And? And? What, Larry?"

I don't know what to say here and I hear myself say, "A date. They were on a date." We had a unit on dating with Mr. Compton, right after the unit on courtesy and table manners.

"A date in the Wilkeses' shed?" I can see in the glowing night that he's confused. "Dates," he says.

We give Witt a minute to climb the baseball diamond backstop.

"Now watch," I tell Rafferty. Witt is going to shine his light at ten o'clock.

"I can't see anything."

"Neither can I." I hold the watch up; we have twenty seconds.

"So, like a date?"

"Yeah, Raff. They're in love." I don't know what I'm saying. The filmstrip on dating showed a guy in a red-checked shirt opening doors for a girl in a blue dress. He shook hands with her father, and then the boy and the girl walked to the school dance. They did not hold hands, because physical contact is not appreciated or necessary, it said, and they both carried the responsibility of initiating conversation. At the dance, they saw their classmates and he got two glasses of the punch. The whole time, every second, even when they were talking or drinking the punch, they were smiling their heads off. They were great smilers. For about a week afterward, I tried to drink things while smiling, and the truth is, I kind of mastered it, though I never did it in public.

We're both staring toward the backstop and I'm reading the watch: Ten.

Five. Four. Three. Two. One.

Witt's flashlight flares once.

"How long did it take?"

"Nothing. Maybe a second."

"You're kidding! From the backstop!"

"Quiet, Rafferty. Wait."

A minute later, at the second, Witt flashes his light again. Then I help blind old Rafferty down through the roof in the dark. We hang from the rafters and drop to the floor of the open structure. This is where the little kids make key chains out of boondoggle and play chess all day long. I made a pair of moccasins here when I was seven years old. Witt is waiting for us at the corner.

"One second," I say to him. "It took maybe one second."

"No," he says. He is walking.

"How long?" Rafferty catches him. The fronts of the houses are all dark as graves.

"No time." He laughs. "The speed of light."

"Yeah, well, we found that out," Rafferty says. "It's faster than the river."

"Yeah, we found that out," Witt says.

We're walking along the glowing street as if nothing has happened, but I feel a little weird. There was something blessed or sinister about Parley and Karen, the understanding between them, her white throat, his wrist where it disappeared, and it all has me riled up and kind of sick. If Parley saw us, or finds out we were there, he'll kill us. Karen Wilkes would never speak to me again. I feel real heavy as we go into Raff's yard and drop on our sleeping bags. Information. I wonder if it's like this for everybody. How does it make you sick?

In the deep night at some thin hour, there is a tremendous *bladdal-ladda*, like that, and Rudy the Warthog appears in the driveway on his belching two-wheeler, which pops two or three times after he dismounts and tramps into the house. The bathroom light goes on and then off. We're all lying still, and in the quiet we can hear the machine sizzling as it settles. I've learned to wait before I respond to events just to make sure they've really occurred, and I hear Rafferty whisper, "Watch this."

He gets up and tiptoes through the dirt to the driveway. In his white jockey shorts he looks like the unfed survivor of some dire event. When he gets over to Rudy's motorcycle, he takes a stance with his feet spread apart, and he lifts his middle finger at the greasy machine. Then he lifts his left hand and does the same thing, pumping both hands up and down in a two-finger salute like a nutty gunman. Witt taps my shoulder and shows me a dirt clod, which he lobs against the garage wall, and when it explodes, Rafferty leaps straight up, spins, and races to us, sliding in. Dust hovers and settles before he pokes his head back out.

"What was that? Did he see me?"

"Does that count?" I ask Witt.

Witt sits up cross-legged on his bag. "Tough call," he says, posing the problem. "Does it count if you flip somebody off and they don't see?"

Rafferty whispers again, urgently, "What was that noise?"

"Could you go around at night and flip off everybody's house?" I ask.

Witt shows Raff another dirt clod and hits the wall again. "Was that what you heard?"

Rafferty sits up. "You shit. And don't tell me that doesn't count. That counts. I went over there in my shorts and gave him both barrels. I could have flipped him off from here." He starts to lift a hand to demonstrate but stops himself just in case.

"And you looked good, believe me," Witt says. "Did you spit on it?"

"No way."

"Then I don't think it counts."

"What!" Rafferty turns to me. "You saw me." He

counts the logic: "I went over. Barefoot. Both fingers. It counts! I flipped him totally off."

Witt counts right back: "Sneaking. In the dark. Quiet as a little mouse. No one sees."

"You saw! It only counts if Rudy sees? That's crazy! That's like saying I can't flip him off without him killing me. If he saw my middle finger, he'd pull it off."

"He'd pull them both off," Witt adds.

"I'm counting it a little," I say. "You did walk over there barefoot."

"I'm not," Witt says. "Think about it. Every time I've flipped my dad off, he's pounded me double. You flip somebody off. They recognize the gesture, and they pound you if they can. That's exactly how you know for sure that it does count."

"This is nuts," Rafferty says. "I didn't need to go over there and risk my life."

"Yes you did," Witt says. "I mean, it looked good and it's a step in the right direction. But it doesn't count."

Rafferty snorts and thrusts his skinny legs back into his bag, twisting away from us.

After a minute, I ask Witt, "How does he catch you to pound you?" I know that Witt's too fast and too wily to be chased down by Budd.

Witt whispers, "I let him. I'm not afraid of him. He can't affect me."

We're quiet a long time, but I don't hear Witt's sleeping breath, which is a kind of *chuff-chuff*, and then later I hear him say to himself, "He can't affect me."

part two

JULY

4 a throwing arm

In combustion, oxygen combines with fuel to produce heat and light. The fuel will begin as a solid or liquid, but it will be vaporized as it burns. The law of conservation of mass-energy dictates that the fuel as it combusts is transformed into an equal amount of light and heat energy, as well as tangible by-products of fire, such as ash and smoke.

The next week, the first week in July, Old Man Wilkes starts burning his shed. After he pulled it over into a heap, he took a long time sorting the broken timbers and the roofing and the glass and nails, and now he comes out every night after dinner, rakes a few more boards into the ash pile back by his alley, and kindles them into flame. He stands above the smoldering fire, always in the same overalls with a grimy, red-flannel shirt, leaning on his charcoaled rake, prodding the boards occasionally, adding a board or two. From time to time, he drags other assorted junk onto the fire—broken chairs, bits of rug, weeds. At this rate, it's going to take him all summer. He's out there every night, a specter with a rake. We never see his wife.

Old Man Wilkes already had a good hatred going for Parley before he caught him in the shed with his daughter. They've been at war since the old man found them kissing on the back step after school and kicked Parley to the property line. Last spring, he drove Karen the three blocks home from school every day, escorting her everywhere, a guard. Karen has been in every class of every grade with me, and I really like her short hair. I voted for her for vice president of the sixth grade; she has great hair to vote for.

Old Man Wilkes has been trying to run Parley over. Witt and Rafferty and I would be walking home from school down Concord, and we'd hear a sharp skid behind us and turn to see the blue Plymouth swerving hard in the gravel and Parley sweeping away up some driveway. The car would slide cockeyed on the street and stay there for a minute, growling. We could see Karen, a defiant prisoner in the passenger seat. No one we have ever seen can run like Parley.

We watch Mr. Wilkes at all times, and when Witt, Rafferty, and I walk past him on our way back from the river, he never looks at us. He simply rakes the ground, adding debris to the little fire. Even unburnable things are dissolving slowly in that smoldering heap.

The World Series of Cup Baseball is interrupted when Mayreen grabs the blue Tupperware cup we are using as a ball and disappears, running around the house. Rafferty had just stroked a line drive, and the cup clipped her in the face where she was standing, experimentally poking Atom with a stick. Witt goes to throw his mitt at her, but she is gone, and he rips around the corner after her, his mitt still aloft in his hand.

We watch the chase and listen for a scream.

"Was that supposed to be a curve?" Rafferty finally asks me.

"I'm not going to tell you."

"Fine. We care. Off the house is a double; that drives in Michelson from third. Six runs in." Rafferty has named his players after neighborhood kids who moved away last year during sixth grade.

"Who hit that?" We're both on our knees looking through our records.

"Bowler."

"Bowler. That tall kid? Did you like him?"

"I liked his electric football game."

"Why'd he move?"

"His father hated the neighborhood. Too many weeds. Too many small fires. Too many kids. Junk like that." Rafferty sits down and starts drumming the broomstick bat against the dented metal pie dish we use as home plate.

Cup Baseball was born the day Atom locked our final tennis ball in his mouth and would not let it go. Witt hated to be forced to quit playing baseball even for two minutes, and he ran into the house. A minute later, he was back with the first of a series of Tupperware cups he would pilfer from his mother's collection. One by one the tumblers have lodged in the rain gutter, forcing us into other pursuits.

Now the game has stopped on this sunny day, and Rafferty and I are sitting in a hole reading our statistics, when we hear a call from the front yard and the blue cup arcs up over the house, falling in the litter of the wrecked backyard. Witt kicks through the side yard and takes his place in center field under the bathroom window.

"Let's go."

I stretch and check second, lean, and deliver: change-up. Rafferty swings way too hard and pops up to shallow right. Witt is there for the out.

As I go to the plate, I see Mayreen march back into the yard. She has not been crying, although Witt has obviously pounded her, as he does every time she takes the cup and runs. Her set mouth and stubborn face are as tough as anything in this neighborhood.

Witt feeds me two fastballs, and I foul off the third. The broomstick doesn't feel right and my confidence is shot. I step out of the box.

"This is Elston Howard," I say, tapping my tennis shoes with the broom handle. "He never strikes out." All my players in Cup are Yankees.

"Yeah, yeah," Witt says, leaning in. He winds up and throws: a slide-spinning curve, too slow. I tap it with the end of the stick in a loopy fly into deep right center.

Witt narrates: "It's going to be off the roof. Rafferty is back to make the catch. Can this guy play it off the roof?"

I watch the cup flip down the shingles, spinning. It tips a standpipe and rolls right into the rain gutter. Rafferty is at the ready under the eave, legs spread, arms up, staring into the sky. He can't see what happened. Mayreen watches him, shaking her head. She is sitting on Atom the sofadog.

Rafferty is a frenzy of readiness.

"On the roof's a triple," I say to Witt. "That puts Howard on third, with Slaughter at the plate." I put Enos Slaughter on my team because his name is etched on my mitt.

"Yeah, well, write it in your book," says Witt. "This game is suspended. I can't take another cup for a few days. Come on, let's hit the pharmacy." As we walk down the alley, we hear Mayreen call to us in her perfect screech, "Eat shit, you slacker bas-tards!"

"Did you teach her that?" Witt says to Rafferty.

At the pharmacy, we are known. As soon as she sees us come in, Denise slides three root beers onto the counter, and she puts all the salt, pepper, sugar, and napkins underneath on a shelf. We spread our raunchy swollen notebooks and start comparing statistics in each of the leagues.

Witt turns through the pages on his clipboard. "Cup's off for at least a week. I'm sick of arguing with Ardean about the cups. He goes on: "Mayreen always tells. It's not worth it."

"She wouldn't tell if you didn't pound her so much."

"If I didn't pound her so much, she'd want to be in

the league, for chrissake!" Witt leans back and spins his stool in disgust.

"You guys wanna play Sock Ball? There's two more games in the regular season." Rafferty tips his mug up and tries to eat the ice before it slides onto the front of his shirt. We play Sock Ball in my yard, using one of Rafferty's socks stuffed hard with grass. Last week, Witt pulled a line drive through the garage window.

"Ah. We better not do that for a while," I say. My father replaced the window right away, and the new glass with its little sticker wrecks the game for me.

We give up on several other games: Liners, too much trouble; Roof Ball, no good place to play; and Fence Ball, for which you need about six players. Wall Ball at Witt's is our best bet, if we can find a ball. Rafferty decides to lower his debts and buys me another root beer so he can have one himself. He's down to ten cents with me, and I'm going to have to swindle him again soon. He stands at the jukebox, debating, but Witt and I know it's going to be "Chopin's Polonaise" and then "Love Me Tender."

"Money to burn," Witt says to me as he gathers his papers and lifts off the stool.

"Hey, not yet," Rafferty says as Witt passes him on his way out. "Piano music is good for your throwing arm."

Behind the pharmacy we rifle the trash for a while and then play Targets. We set up the big glass pop-syrup bottle and each take three throws. It's always a short game, and in the second round Rafferty smashes the bottle. The crash is followed by the sound of the metal back doors opening, and we run down the alley, clutching our record books.

"Nice arm," Witt says. "You should listen to more piano music."

"Let's see if Atom has a tennis ball and play Wall."

"He's eaten them all by now."

"Look." I point down the alley. We can see the white-gray smoke cross the sky. "Old Man Wilkes is starting early."

"That guy's a menace."

The summer hangs above us like the exploding billows of the trees along the alley. Every single thing is growing. All the green in this world of four blocks, three streets, two alleys, one park, the river, and Witt's yard grows its own wild way, spearing through asphalt, eating fences, and leaping into the bright air like a jungle on fire. The air itself swims with fifty million mingling smells. Walking buoyantly down the alley with my two friends, I take a deep breath and love this day, the exact high rich center of summer, this feeling that something will happen.

We find Atom in his favorite burrow in Witt's yard. Laid out like a cheap dog doormat, he looks dead. The WITT in smudged white letters is still legible on his side. In his mouth, jailed behind four rotten fangs, is a tennis ball.

I lift the deadweight of Atom's head and try to pry his jaws apart. No way. I peel back the black lips until a line of pink shows inside each slimy gum. I've had my hands in this dog's mouth a hundred times. We spent one day throwing wild new pitches by smearing a ball with his oily saliva, and then we quickly moved to outlaw its use in any of our games. Atom looks at me now as if he is not involved in this. His breath smells like things we have turned over down at the river.

"This'll do it." I put my hands over his nostrils and smile up at Rafferty and Witt, trying not to inhale. A minute passes. "He's got to breathe!"

"Wanna bet!" Rafferty says. "This is no normal dog. Stop up his ears, too."

I drop Atom's head and it falls back against the dirt bank. I look to Witt. "You wanna cut it out?" Without moving, the dog rolls his eyes at me and lets the ball emerge from his mouth.

"Hey, Witt," I say, lifting the wet, black tennis ball in two fingers. "Hey, Atom left it."

In his announcer's voice Witt calls, "Play ball."

Wall Ball is a tough game, but it is a great game. It has everything. The batter faces the wall of the house, the pitcher *behind* him, the fielder *behind* him out farther in the yard. The pitcher tosses the ball against the house; it bounds back through the hitter's strike zone and he clobbers it *wham!* off the wall and it rebounds into the field. The total advantage of Wall Ball is that it can be played full speed, no choke up, no soft throws, in a tenth of the space required for Strike Out or Liners.

After huddling to compare our record books to see where we were, I end up at the plate with Rafferty on the mound. Witt is out in the yard somewhere, hiding in a hole. It is his strategy as a fielder in Wall Ball to conceal himself so the batter won't know where to push the ball.

"Come on, Witt!" I cry.

"No way!" his voice calls from the thicket. "Hit the ball!"

Rafferty has a distracting windmill windup that I try

to ignore, and he delivers straight overhand. The tennis ball, black as an eight ball, lobs up and falls sharply through my swing: strike one. It's the best pitch in Wall: the slow drop. However, because the ball is still wet from Atom's mouth, I can see the spot on the wall where Rafferty threw it, and I move closer, four feet. The neighbors would think I am about to attack the house with a broomstick. There are five or six patches chipped out of the wooden shingle siding where that has happened. That's what is great about Witt's place; his parents don't care that from time to time we hit the house with sticks.

Witt's dad Budd wrecked the front of the house himself. One night last year he missed the driveway and swung the fender of the Buick right through the corner of Mayreen's room, blasting a hole in the house and dragging Mayreen's quilt and stuffed elephant right into the night with the edge of the bumper. We were sleeping out that night and ran around to the front to see Budd climb out of the car and trip in the quilt. He got up and poked his head up into the fresh creaking fissure to see if Mayreen was all right and to stuff the elephant and the quilt back into the cavity.

It's a pretty neat hole, big enough for Witt to sneak out of. In the winter Mayreen packed it with blankets, and now in the summer it gapes at the world like a sad mouth, shocked that people could live this way. Every few days Atom grapples into the opening and slithers through the house, eating everybody's candy.

Rafferty winds and pitches, another slow drop. I step close to the house, swinging almost straight up. Contact! The black ball rips back up the wall, popping high into shallow center. I tear for the porch and see Witt as he breaks through the four-foot brambles and dives, tassels of weed litter flying from his hair. He makes the catch, narrating all the time: ". . . off his shoestrings, ladies and gentlemen. We have it on the replay and it is not a trapped ball, but a great play by an out-stand-ing center fielder. . . ."

We rotate. I'm in the weeds and Rafferty's at the plate. Witt's pitching specialty is the ricocheting fastball. Witt is in the middle of his figure-eight windup when Parley comes around the corner of the house. Witt's yard is the most prominent shortcut in the neighborhood. Parley's presence changes the day, charges us. He's our hero, but there's a chance that he's here to kill us. Witt unwinds and says, "Hey, Parley, where you going?" Parley looks high; something's going on. I can tell by the way he keeps his chin tilted up. I check the side of the house to see if

Old Man Wilkes is lurking around.

"Hello, boys." Relief strikes me like a board across the back of my legs, and I sit down in the dirt. He doesn't know we were at the Wilkeses' shed, any of it.

"We got a rock fight over by Lopez's. Those guys from Riverside want a rock fight. We could use some help." He flips his hand out in a wave and jogs up the alley, looking both ways just in case the Murder Plymouth is cruising hereabouts.

Witt sits down on the rippled-tin home plate. Rafferty walks in from the pitcher's mound, and I step over to them. Parley's gone, apparently to a rock fight.

"You guys want to go over to the rock fight or finish the game?"

"You think we ought to go?"

"You want to?"

"Parley's down there. And those guys from Riverside are always a pain."

"We know that, Rafferty."

"Rock fight," Witt says.

"I don't much want to go to a rock fight," I say, tossing the ball left hand to right hand. "What do they do?"

"It's rocks, I guess."

"I don't care," Rafferty says. "We could finish the

game later. We never finish any game."

"Yeah," Witt says, standing up. "We gotta go over." Since we are still sitting there, he adds, "Don't you think?"

I stand up and hand the ball to Witt. "Yeah," I say. "I guess."

Rafferty stands up.

Witt tosses the black tennis ball over to where Atom lies in his ditch playing dead, so we'll know where to find it later.

Going to the rock fight, I feel sick. My stomach feels very heavy, pounds and pounds. We walk ten feet apart: Witt, then me, then Rafferty. It's as if we are being dragged by a chain. We don't talk all the way past the pharmacy, and Witt finally stops and points out, "Better get some rocks." We kneel in the gravel and fill our pockets with walnut-size rocks.

"What do they do?" I say. "Like is there a charge and then they charge back, or what?"

"I don't know."

"Why do they have a rock fight?" Rafferty says.

Parley is leaning on Lopez's fence, talking to Benny and Cling.

"Three guys," I whisper to Witt. "They've got three guys?"

"Six now. And Cling counts for two."

"Hey, Parley," Rafferty says. Everybody nods at everybody else. Parley's chin is still way out there. Then we don't know what to do; there's no more room on the fence. Finally we sit on the ditch bank. The clump of rocks in my pocket gouges at my leg; this is so obviously a mistake.

"Hey, Benny. Hey," I say to Cling. I cannot say his name. He is dangerous; he barks at cars. You never see him on the same bike twice. He's got a tattoo on his neck, the left side. It's just a circle, but every time I see it I think of a bolt and wonder just how his head is fastened on. I'm scared of Cling.

When I was six or seven, Cling grabbed me one day when I was headed home from summer crafts. He pushed me down and stood above me, the insole of each boot against one of my ears. He plucked the key chain I was making for my mother, a pink and green weave of boondoogle, and pulled it apart in three quick tugs, dropping it onto my face. His empty hand was out to collect cigarette money, and as I squirmed to reach the nickel and the dime in my pocket, he threatened to spit down upon me. He was the one person in the world that when I saw him, I went the long way around, and now we're allied in a rock war. I look at him sideways, and I realize that he doesn't know who I am. He doesn't remember that fifteen cents he owes me.

Benny comes over and collapses on the grass. A slash of black hair falls across his eyes. He and Cling are the only guys we know who smoke. "You guys ready?"

Witt says, "Sure." I shrug a *who knows*, which means *not really*. Benny sharpens the hot cone of his cigarette on a blade of grass and speaks from way back in his throat. "Throw low, that's all you gotta do. Get it to skip off the road." He leans back on an elbow and gurgles a low laugh. "Throw low. Bother them."

My throat is closed and I cannot swallow. I sit stock-still, though I am slowly turning inside out in a very sickening way. Parley leans against the fence like a young cowboy, lean and loose, ready to rock fight. Though this is a bad deal from top to bottom, I'm thinking way deep down that I have a good arm. I've always had a good arm and can hit any tree trunk from across the street.

Then we hear the call from the corner of Furbish's alley. It's a tall kid named Chambers, and he wants to talk to Parley. Parley pushes himself up off the fence, lazily, and takes those long strides out over the street, into the field, which is no-man's-land, to the mouth of the alley.

"They don't got nobody," Cling says. But I can see a number of shirts behind Chambers. Eight, nine, ten. Parley walks right up to all of them, straight up, and talks to Chambers. From here I can see his hands in his back pockets. Then I see him point back at us and draw a line with his hand between the two groups.

"What's going on?" Rafferty says, peering in the general direction of the field. Rafferty does things in the general direction without his glasses; that's why he's really no threat in Cup or Wall. Or a rock fight.

"Nothing yet, except that big rock sailing right at your head," Witt says.

"Is it started? Are they really gonna have it?"

I stand up, placing my hand over the bulging rocks in my pocket. I don't want any of the other gang to see them and consider me dangerous, or even vaguely hostile. I stand on one leg hoping I can be interpreted—from their distance—as being simply some dumb guy who came over to watch. I know if there weren't six of us, there would be no fight; we should never have come.

What really makes me ache is the way Parley lifts his chin and smiles and points at Chambers before he turns and walks slowly across the field and back across the road to us.

"Yeah?" Benny asks.

Parley smiles. "It's just Chambers and some assholes from Riverside."

"Yeah?"

"They'll stay in the field. We'll stay on the road. That's it." Benny salutes Parley with a jagged piece of quartzite.

"How many guys they got?" Witt asks Parley.

"A few."

Chambers disappears into the huddle of his gang and then dances out of the alley ahead of the pack of at least a dozen kids. I can't count, I'm so sick. They spread and mill about the field.

"Let's go," Parley says. "Kick some ass."

I can't move. I've never been in a fight. I've never even heard of a rock fight. Witt and Rafferty stand and move up onto the old road where Cling and Benny hunker. Their hands dangle full of rocks, waiting for the signal. I hear Rafferty say to Witt, "Okay, okay, no problem. I can see them. I can see where they are."

Behind me a block and a half is my own home. I could be sitting in the old swing set dragging my shoes in the dirt. I should really spend more time at home. I'm surprised as I shift my weight to see my feet move forward, out onto the street. I feel exactly like someone else, someone I don't know and don't like very much. This is one more thing I'm going to have to lie to my mother and father about; they deserve a better kid. They should have had Keith Gurber. When I move into our line beside Rafferty, I hear myself say, "Rafferty and Witt— you bastards." There is a rock in my throwing hand: my other hand is full, too.

"Do we get a couple of throws to warm up?" Witt says, and Parley laughs. Over our heads Old Man Wilkes's shed drifts as a gray rash of smoke; the whole world is doom.

Chambers suddenly runs out to the edge of the field, thirty feet from Parley, and he stands there dancing like a boxer. The rock in his right hand is the size of a coffee cup.

"Parley!"

"Yeah, Chambers."

"You're a fucking asshole and you smell like shit!"

"Is that it?" Parley sounds bored.

"You're a pussy, shithead!"

Parley stands, one hand in a pocket, his feet spread,

his head cocked over. He looks at Chambers with nothing but flat curiosity.

"Well?" Chambers yells. "What do you think of that, Parley Shithead?"

"I hate to kill you for that trite shit." I've never heard anyone say the word *trite* before. I think that: I had to wait for a rock fight to hear the word *trite*.

This sets Chambers off, and he runs clear back to Furbish's alley to encourage his troops, yelling and pulling at the shirts of his gang members. I can feel a hard raining of rocks at any minute. Then Chambers stops, he thumbs his jeans back up around his waist, and he walks back toward us. He is really built; clearly he is strong enough to kill us all. He is skipping and wheeling closer and closer, and suddenly he wings his rock, an asteroid, and it roars across the street, ripping a vacuum in the afternoon, missing Benny by an inch and crashing into the old link fence like a rocket. At the edge of the road, Chambers stops and says quietly to Parley, "Karen Wilkes eats it raw."

I don't see Parley throw. I suspect it is his sidearm sling, which has no visible windup or backswing; it just whips forward with a swift side snap of the elbow and then the wrist: *flick*. I do see the flat rock he hurls rise and take Chambers in the neck, just below the jaw-bone, and tip his head back in a wicked snap so that he staggers and then steps out nowhere, into air, and falls on his face like a sack of cement.

No one moves for a minute, not even Chambers. Then a howl rises from him, cracking as he turns and begins to roll in pain. The little gang folds from the back, retreating into the alley as Cling throws boulders at them as fast as he can. Witt, Rafferty, and I have not really moved.

"Where'd they go?" Rafferty says. Witt looks behind him at me with a full, frank look of relief on his face. Their gang has left Chambers on his back, groaning at the sky. I see Parley go to him and bend over, and then I note that I am right behind him; I want to see the effect of the rock and I want to see Chambers's face, the pain. As Witt grabs my belt and pulls me back, I have the strangest feeling and it thrills me: I want to kick Chambers. A couple of times. What is happening to me? We start walking to Witt's, and Parley turns to us and points. He's grinning.

Ambling up the alley, we explain to Rafferty what happened. He nods excitedly. We're all high, high from having our lives spared, our bodies intact. I still have a pocket full of rocks. I'm considering taking them home as souvenirs, putting them on my bookcase. Rafferty keeps repeating, "Those suckers sure can run, right?" Then he laughs and laughs.

"Let's cut through Haslams' yard and catch those guys before they get back to Riverside," I say. I punctuate it by throwing a rock into the back of Smalls' sheds, where it comes off the tin like a gunshot.

"Larry's temporarily insane," Witt says, and he's jogging for home.

We're flying when we cruise into the back lot at Witt's house. My ears are roaring, and I'm shot with that high happiness in my lungs that means I better not laugh because I could cry. But there's another new taste in my mouth, and I know that I wanted to fight. Witt pushes Rafferty into the geothermal pit and then helps him climb out, and then we find the ball where we left it, untouched by Atom, but we are too pumped to play Wall Ball or anything else. We're just not on the ground.

Witt throws a couple of rocks over Smalls', three, four, five, until we hear glass break, and we dive into the large foxhole and hide, muffling our racing laughter in the weeds. We've gone crazy.

"Gee, Witt, Old Man Smalls is going to kick our

asses!" Rafferty says. Witt is too giddy to listen; besides, we've had worse. Glass breaks every day in this neighborhood. He rolls onto his back, his mouth pursed but heaving in laughter, and he arches to get his hand in his pocket so he can extract another rock. His face still buckling, he holds the rock before our faces with two fingers, as if it were a coin, and then still from the sitting position, he throws it up in a soft lob right through his own bathroom window. The crash is flat and obvious, a sound so wonderfully wrong that Rafferty convulses and jumps up to run away. He's afraid adults are going to be involved in this mayhem soon. Witt tackles him in his first step and starts yelling, "He did it! Rafferty did it!" It is hard to understand what he is saying. Or doing. "Rafferty is responsible!" Witt makes the word *responsible* sound like it has twelve parts that don't exactly fit, like the funniest word of all time. Rafferty is on his back, almost upside down in the geothermal pit, with Witt on top of him. Witt has stopped trying to call out; he has become a soggy bag of laughter.

Mayreen screams from the broken window. Her face framed in the jagged broken glass is a fist of indignation. "You animals! You slimy assholes!"

Witt and Rafferty stop wrestling and look at this

freckled banshee, wailing out the window. It is as if she is the face of the wrecked old house, and she goes on and on, "Waaaaaaahh-aaaaaaah!" She learned the word *slimy* from Budd. When the mouth closes, so Mayreen can breathe and swallow and allow her eyes to close, Witt says quietly, from where he and Rafferty now sit on the bank of a trench, "Oh, shut up."

5 car baseball

The principles of any good game can be variously applied to other conditions and circumstances to create heretofore uninvented ventures and contests and challenges. A game depends on its set of rules. Game theory deals with the probability of outcomes.

When the sun falls below Smalls' sheds, it is time for me to go home and check in and have dinner. When I cross Concord Avenue, my father is rounding the park in his green Chevrolet pickup, and he slows so I can step onto the bumper plate like a fireman. I love the two-block ride, the wind taking my hair, my arms stretched straight before me, my hands gripping the tailgate. Mr. Wilkes is always out at this time, working his fire, and my father honks once and waves.

"Always wave at Mr. Wilkes," he tells me. "He's one of our neighbors."

"He never waves back."

"That doesn't matter. He knows what a wave is and he appreciates it."

So, I, too, lift a hand toward Mr. Wilkes, who turns his head up a moment and stirs his pile again.

Mr. Wilkes has become serious about burning the parts of his torn-down shed. From our dinner table every night, we can see him across the vacant lot, raking debris onto the smoking pile, constantly moving while the gray smoke falls out down the alley. The old lumber doesn't really smell too bad at a block and a half; the wood smoke laced with weedy residue is the smell of my neighborhood.

"Poor old coot," my father says. "He could haul it all to the dump in one trip. I should probably offer to help him."

But I know better. Mr. Wilkes has a pickup like everybody else in our neighborhood. It's a pale brown International. Mr. Wilkes doesn't want to haul his shed away to the dump. He wants to be outside, burning it so that the smoke can rise through this neighborhood like a warning: DON'T TOUCH MY DAUGHTER. And: I'M GOING

TO KILL YOUNG PARLEY. He rakes and rakes in the smol-dering dusk.

At dinner in my house, we are asked to account for our day. My brothers, being six and three, have smaller accounts and derail the conversation with their creative table manners. This used to work for me, too. My mother serves the dinner: potatoes and peas, which my brothers don't have to eat if they don't want, and some kind of meat, and she sits down. My mother and father talk to each other in an easy way. My mother speaks happily, her voice arch and wry as she goes over my brothers' flub-ups. I know my parents will talk for a while, and then one of them will turn to me and ask me to account for my day. I try to fill my mouth slowly and completely as my mother is wrapping up her report, so that I can chew until the topic passes, which it has done at times. But I know I am not going to avoid my turn tonight. I chew and chew and try to think of what to say. How I wish I was their own true son, instead of this spy loaded with secrets and ready to lie. I am not going to mention losing another of Witt's mother's cups in the rain gutter, or that Witt beat up his sister with a weed, or that he threw a rock right through his bathroom window today—on purpose—or that I was in a rock fight and there was a hot sliver of me that wanted it, liked it.

"Played ball," I say.

"All day?"

"Pretty much."

"Where at?"

"Down at Witt's."

"Did they ever fix that hole in Mayreen's room?"

"Not yet." I am not surprised anymore when my parents read my mind. I expect a rock fight question at any minute.

"Wouldn't take much to fix that," my father says, and I can see he's already thinking about the whole thing. It comes up once a week: the neighborhood. "There's another car dumped in front of Harpers'," he says, looking out the window. Without moving his head, he can see three abandoned vehicles: two in the vacant lot and one behind the Wilkeses'. Throughout the neighborhood, there are dozens of lost cars, most of them right side up, missing wheels, rusting. If you grow up here, you don't even see them, but once in a while and more frequently these days, they are leaping into my father's view. He doesn't want to live in a parking lot for the dead.

My father pushes his chair away from the table. Then he frowns and clucks disappointment at the world outside the window. As he rises, he smiles and leans forward to twist Eddie's ear lightly as a joke. Eddie is stirring his ice cream into a creamy paste; it's his favorite way to eat it. My father stands behind me a moment pretending my head is a leaning post. His hand is as big as a baseball mitt. "He could haul all that mess away with one load." He leans on me playfully, and for this one minute I will not let him down. I draw a slow breath, a deep breath. Dinner is over, and I have not ruined our household with any hideous news. Outside, the smoke begins to merge with the first purple skies of the great never-ending summer twilight.

I see Rafferty straggle toward my house through the vacant lot. He is walking backward, dragging his tattered sleeping bag, watching Mr. Wilkes. I don't know how Rafferty can be here already; he must never get any dinner. We have worked out a system for asking permission to sleep out; I tell my parents that Witt's parents will let him if I can or that Rafferty's mother will let him if they let me. In reality, Witt just slips away, and Rafferty says he can sleep out any time he wants without asking because his mother has company so much, meaning Rudy the Crude. Mornings when Rafferty sleeps here, he eats bowls and bowls of cereal. Rafferty eats dinner with us too sometimes, but my father disapproves, not of sharing what we have with him, but of not giving Rafferty's family a chance to share dinner with him. When we're in our yard at supper time, Dad will call, "Come in, boys," to my brothers and me. To Rafferty he will add, "And Rafferty, you go home. Your mother just called—she's got a prize for you." Years ago, when he first started that, Rafferty and Witt would fall for it and race away.

Now Rafferty crosses into our yard as I step outside to meet him.

"Old Man Wilkes is a long-term weirdo." Rafferty is still looking over there. I know he can't see the dark figure of Mr. Wilkes; he must just be smelling the smoke. "If I grow up and tear my shed down and burn it day by day, I hope somebody puts me away."

"What about chasing kids with your car, trying to run them down?"

"Yeah." Rafferty turns to me at last. "Well, that part might not be too bad!" Rafferty gathers up his sleeping bag from where he's dragged it on the ground and leads me into our backyard, where he throws it against the fence. I like that about him: he may be nearsighted, but he still acts like king of the Gypsies. He sits down and opens his statistics notebook.

"Look at this," he says. He's made a three-color crayon chart of all of his hitters in Wall Ball. I sit down with him to go over his batting averages and wait for Witt.

When you lie back on your sleeping bag after sunset in my neighborhood, the last thing you see in the sky before the stars appear is the haze of Mr. Wilkes's shed burning. Sometimes we stretch out and have first-star contests, where we stare up so hard and so long that smoke lifts us slowly in its trance. It can make you dizzy, drifting like that. Then we have to blink hard, clench our eyes, and start again, so that it is again the smoke moving and not the Earth. If you really want to play well, you should turn on an elbow and look west, because Venus will pop right out even in the blue-black and spoil the whole contest. A sitting duck.

Rafferty and I are on our backs, floating in the twilight, when Witt sneaks across the field and rakes the fence so hard with a stick that Rafferty cries out and throws his hands across his face to protect himself from the crashing Plymouth.

Witt wears a high grin, an expression he always has after slipping away from home at night. Budd expects

Witt to stay home and, being the oldest, protect the property, such as it is. But as soon as Ardean calls him in, Witt answers, goes down the hall into Mayreen's room, and slips out through the hole in the house. He squirms out headfirst, jumps on his waiting bike, and careens that mechanism down to my house.

Witt grins, unfurls his sleeping bag, and flops down. "Go ahead: M.M."

"Easy as ice cream," Rafferty says. "Mickey Mantle."

"Don't be stupid."

"Mickey Mouse."

"Marilyn Monroe."

"Now we hope that you guys will dig just a bit deeper." He turns on his back and calls, "Dibbs!" pointing at Venus, which has just now broken through. "Four nights in a row!" Witt slaps his own hands. "Hit it, you guys." His grin is wicked, and he tosses a pointed finger at our swing set, the one my dad made.

Rafferty shakes his head. I don't understand him all of the time; he has difficulty believing that he regularly gets beaten in a game that requires good vision. I guess you call it a good attitude. But Witt has won, so we strip down to our shorts and race around the swings and back. Rafferty does a broad hook slide into his sleeping bag, crying, "Heeeee's saaffffffe!"

"I don't think Venus should count," I say to Witt.

"Oh, why don't we change the rules every time we lose."

"Hey, I ran already. I just don't think you should be able to use the same star twice."

Witt closes his mouth, twists one corner up and one corner down, and finally says, "M.M."

"Yeah, yeah," Rafferty says. "We'll get it."

At full dark, my father comes out of the house. He leans on the fence and talks to my friends. I realize he is the only parent in the whole neighborhood who talks to the kids. He guesses Mitch Miller when he hears of the game, and he stands to go in, looking over our heads at the dark world. Sometimes I wonder what he is thinking, but he just says, "Now settle down, boys," and goes in the house.

The nights we sleep at Witt's, no one comes out to see us, and we make camp way back past the small ditch in the weeds. Early in the summer, I can barely stand to sleep down there; the smell of the weeds is so powerful it seems dangerous. All night the house rumbles, rocking with light and a variety of bangings. One night as we lay suffocating in the underbrush, I heard a crash and rose to my elbows to see a man fall out of the back of the house, followed closely by a flying shovel and then Budd. The man ran around and around the old Hudson racked on blocks in the driveway while Budd tried to strike him with the flat side of the shovel. Inside the house, Witt's mother Ardean could be heard singing. Finally I saw Budd plunge the shovel through the rear window of the car, where it lodged, regardless of how he tried to yank it around. The other man sat on the fender and laughed, and the last thing I saw before I ducked was Budd and that guy laughing and sitting on the sad, old, green car.

That night, Rafferty woke up and said to me, "What's going on?"

"Nothing. More murder. Go back to sleep."

Once Dad has gone inside, we wait for the signal, the bathroom light going off, and we start with the real game: Car Baseball. It always starts the same. We're talking, arguing about how many different triple plays are possible, when suddenly Witt is gone, running for the swing set. He tags the swings and races back to his bag, sliding in just before the car, which we hadn't noticed, passes before us on Derby Street.

"Man on first."

He's got a single on us, and Rafferty is up, his hands in the fence, his head swiveling both ways down Derby. I love him for his useless activities. He couldn't see a car if it was falling on him.

A car turns off Concord, too close, and we all try for it. I know it is just too tight, the kind of car we wouldn't run on later in the game. In a straight race I'm faster than Witt, and I hit the swings first and turn for the bags, sliding in safe just as the lights pass. I turn to see Witt flat on his back in a full slide.

"Tie goes to the runner." He points at me. "Runners on first and second."

Rafferty slides in halfway back, ten feet off the base, as a joke, and he walks up. "One down," he says. "I always start slow."

Rafferty is canny at Car Baseball, and when he sees a dull glow way down beyond Seventh South, he calls, "I'm going on that one." If it turns away and fails to pass us, he's out. He's running back and forth to the swings. Once, a single; twice, a double. As he touches his bag, he says, "He's going for three." The lights persist, and when they pass Wasatch Avenue, Witt and I join Rafferty, who is going for a home run. He makes it standing up, as do we. But it's only a single for us. Standing with his hands on his knees, Rafferty breathes: "One out, but one *in*. I'm going for the record!"

"Sixty-four," Witt says. But he doesn't have to. We all know the record. It's Parley's record, set one night when he didn't want to go home and came by to harass us for a while. Sixty-four runs with a man left on second, and Parley walked away with only one out. Parley can run like terror.

Sixty-four runs is going to be a tough record to crack on Derby Street. The uneven traffic only holds for an hour or two after dark, then it's one car an hour except on special nights. We stand by the fence and hope for cars. Witt has the bases loaded; I've got two on, but for now, Rafferty has the lead.

I'm a conservative player, but so is Witt, and I know that my hope of catching him tonight is by going for singles on cars making the quick turn off Concord. Sometimes we can see the car lights in reflection off the stop sign, and if I run on speculation that it will turn our way, I can nab a double while everyone else watches.

By ten o'clock, we begin to hear the railroad trains whining their awesome harmonics as they drag the very world away, and the game of Car Baseball is full tilt.

Rafferty: twenty runs, runner on second, one out.

Witt: twenty-nine runs, bases loaded, no outs.

Me: twenty-seven runs, runners at first and third, no outs.

We are all standing, fingers in the fence, on our toes, ready to push off and steal a step on the other two. Rafferty holds his head in such a way that I can tell he is listening as hard as he is staring down Derby. Every so often, Witt rattles the fence, and we watch Rafferty take off, springing four steps before he finds us not with him, and he stops, turns, and walks back with a kind of dignity. "Very funny," he says. We are ready to fly when Rafferty says, "Listen!"

"What have you got, Rafferty? A tank coming?"

"Listen!"

We stand and look at the ground, listening. I can hear something and then it is clear in the night: Parley's voice. I can't hear all the words, but he sounds hurried, and if I didn't know better, scared. Then I can hear him say, "No! This way! No! No!" Then a slam and then another greater concussion.

There is a car coming, but Witt just sits on his sleeping bag, and so I sit down and let the car drive by. If you let a car pass, it's a strike. We don't hear anything more from across the lot, but we're staring. I see a shape move across a small light. "Look!"

"What?" Rafferty says. "Can you see him?"

Two headlights ignite in the Wilkeses' yard. They're huge beacons, so I know it's Mr. Wilkes in his Plymouth. Then, right across the lights, full front, I see Parley's X-ray form pass and disappear on the run. The headlights spin, close together, cross eyed, and I hear the old growl of that terrible car as it swings out onto the street. Another car runs around the Concord corner and in front of us before we move. "Strike two," Rafferty says. "Right?"

He gets up. Witt and I do, too, but Witt says, "Something's going on." We both know it is not right that Old Man Wilkes would be up so late. Suddenly, in fact, everything is beginning to seem late.

"He's going to kill Parley," Rafferty says. It sounds pretty bad the way he says it: information. "But I'm going on Old Man Wilkes. This is going to put me back in the ball game."

It almost does. We watch the Plymouth clear across the field. It's swinging through the stop signs, cruising for murder, and Rafferty only has time to nab a double—and he has to hit the dirt with that. Witt and I duck as the old Plymouth sweeps by; we take the strike.

"Strike three, boys," Rafferty says. "It's one out all

around. How can you guys strike out like that?"

Witt is biting his lower lip.

"There's nothing we can do, Witt," I say. "Parley's okay; he can run."

Witt stands with his fists in the fence. He turns to me, "Twenty-nine runs, bases loaded, *one* out." And he's gone, running for the swings on a car I finally see, coming down from Nevada Avenue. He takes a double to my single, and we all settle to the game.

Witt takes off his shoes and his shirt and poses as a sprinter, one fingertip touching the fence. The cars are backed up at the Seventh South stop sign; we'll be running for a long time tonight. The air is bright, and the Milky Way is so thick it looks like smoke.

On a fine, strange night after a day of baseball and a rock fight, on a night so strange it is like night on another planet, with your shoes off running in the new dew, with bare feet at an hour that is so far beyond late that it is no time, on a night like that, a person can run a long time. It is no trouble. The car lights swing onto your street, and you fly around for a while, back and forth, doubles, triples, home runs, sliding in safely as each car passes. The bright night air will sparkle in your throat when you slide on your back, and you won't remember standing again, being ready, and launching at the next lights, trying and making a double into a triple, sliding again, your bare back against the grass where that electric itch will grow like burning wings as you fly into the next run.

We've always hid from cars, always. It is among my deepest impulses. No one taught it to us, and it didn't start as a game or anything external, just as some true reflex. It happened the first time I was out after dark, this hiding, and my earliest memories of seeing car lights coming from any direction on any street always feature someone whispering harshly, "Car!" and the rest of us kids ducking and scattering into the bushes, behind the porch, flat in the thick grass, anywhere out of those lights.

But I've never run so fast as I am running tonight. Every twenty minutes Old Man Wilkes grinds by looking for Parley; when we see the car coming, we rocket back and forth, trying for triples. Old Man Wilkes is going to put a hundred miles on his car tonight, just driving six blocks.

Every half hour we see the blazing shadow of Parley run through the lot or down Concord, always on the edge of lights. He runs like a god. Seeing him, I feel the hair on my neck rise in sweet fear. Suddenly he appears outside the fence, not even breathing hard.

"Hey, boys. Nice work at the rock fight."

"Hey, Parley."

"This guy was dying to throw a rock, weren't you?" He points at me. "You guys playing Car Baseball?"

I want to say: *Parley, is Old Man Wilkes really going to kill you?*

Parley pulls lightly at the scar on his left ear. "How many runs in?"

I want to say: *Run, Parley, I'm scared for you.*

"Thirty-eight," Rafferty says. "Witt has got forty-seven. It's a good night."

A car turns off Nevada and cruises our way. Parley lets it come a block and the lights start to rise on his face. As the car passes Concord, continuing, we see the boatlike expanse of the old Plymouth loom in the streetlight. Parley stands straight up and cocks his head. "Well, who's got the record?" he asks, though it's not really a question, and he leaps into a sprint right across the path of the car and is gone into the vacant lot. We all fall to our bags and hide, taking the strike.

When it is quiet and dark again, Rafferty says, "If Mr. Wilkes doesn't go home, we're going to have to run all night."

"So will Parley."

I can feel Parley and that Plymouth orbiting the neighborhood, pulling sounds and shapes out of the night sky, and for the three of us, Witt, Rafferty, and me, there is no rest. On the next sure single off Nevada Avenue, Rafferty turns right into me as we're at the swings, and we both go down in a pile on the grass as the car whips past; out number two for both of us. We're barely able to limp back to our sleeping bags before the next car passes: strike one. Rafferty's lip is bleeding where it hit my head. While we're moaning, Witt makes a double home run (legal) on a car that inches along the vacant lot, looking for something, we guess. A Car Baseball dream car; so slow and so straight.

Rafferty takes his third out on a long shot, which stops a hundred yards up the road and pulls over to park. When the lights go out, Rafferty collapses on his bag and moans. He was up to forty-two runs. I've seen him draw the third out ten times, but never with forty-two runs. There's a chance he may cry. But suddenly he's up, the old Rafferty. He says to us, "No outs, no runs." He's starting over. He runs with us, as wired as before, for five more runs, when suddenly that parked car jumps to life. The lights flash and the car springs past us before we can even take a step. Rafferty is saved! An out becomes a double for him. He's back in it at forty-seven runs, man on second, and he's talking all the time, tighter and higher than I've ever seen him.

"That is total skill." He's laughing. "Take the chance; have the faith."

"Yeah, you're a genius at this game," Witt says. "I wonder what makes some guy park with a date for four minutes." He shakes his head.

It is clearly later, stranger, than we've ever played this game. I've sneaked in three singles when I caught Witt standing, but otherwise it's all neck and neck. He's two runs in the lead: 55 to 53. My runners are at second and third.

As I stand ready, waiting for cars, I stare across the lot, past the dark hulks of the abandoned cars, hoping to see Mr. Wilkes pull into the yard and end tonight's rampage. We've all made twelve or fifteen runs off his car alone, but it is enough. We want him to go home now. I've run so much I'm dizzy. Sometimes one of us sits, taking two strikes before rising and nailing a single, then sitting again. Late, late into the night there is a long, long period of no cars, and then a short period of cars all in a hurry, rounding the corners wide, racing away. And then the whole night changes and I realize I've never been up so late before in my life. The dark is thicker than it was, the few stars now fuzzy.

I run hard for a double on some kind of truck, a van, and slide onto my bag easily—sliding is like dreaming—when we hear a strange noise rising from down Concord Street. At first I think the sound, so raw and magnified, might just be in my head, but then I see Witt's face, up listening in the small starlight, and the screeching of metal rises all around us. The Plymouth. It sounds like a train wreck. Then there is a *whump! whump!* and we feel the earth shudder as Concord Street explodes in a shower of sparks. The streetlight cries and collapses over the stop sign and cartwheels like a thrown torch, once, twice, into the vacant lot. Our eyes are split open by the flash, but in the yawning dark, I think there is something in the air, a figure flying: Parley. He sails through the smoky air above Derby Street and on into the darkness of the ruined vacant lot. It's like I'm dreaming: I swear he flies by in slow motion. And next, a series of sparks skitters out along the asphalt, and the Plymouth, lights out, surges past the Concord corner. It, too, is off the roadway. Wheels agoggle, the car heaves across, arched so high that we can see the undercarriage. A ragged fire rides along the muffler. It all passes us like a spaceship and is swallowed by blackness. My eyes can't take it. I close them and listen, but no crash comes. There is some hissing and then that dies, but no crash comes. It is as if nothing has come down.

"Holy shit!" Rafferty says. "What was that?"

Witt flashes me a quick look. He sits down on his bag and starts rubbing his eyes, like Rafferty. I lie down on mine. "I don't know," I say to Rafferty. "Old Man Wilkes is still chasing him." This is all a bad dream. I can't swallow and my eyes burn even closed.

"It looked like that to me," Witt says real quietly.

"What a night!" Rafferty says.

"What is that?" I hear later. "Witt, what is that?" I wake knowing what it is: the acrid cinder smoke from Mr. Wilkes's shed fire. I roll over. Across the field, the fire is starting again. "Have there been any cars?"

"That guy has flipped right out."

"Naw, he's not even there. You know what time it is? That fire started by itself."

The sky has changed into something I've never seen before: not night, not day; too dark to see, too light not to try. And through everything, the heavy smell of smoke.

"Have there been any cars?"

"None."

"Are we still playing?"

But Witt and Rafferty are gone, running on a station wagon, and I follow them to a single. The three trails from our bags to the swings are distinct in the small, strange, gray light. After that, it picks up. We run on several people we know who are going to work. We run on the garbage truck, though it feels unfair because we know where it's going and it goes real slow.

Across the way, the fire swells into a yellow blossom as big as a milk truck. And in front of it, passing through it like a pendulum, is the wavering silhouette of Mr. Wilkes. Outlines of the wrecks in the weed field are rising through the new light. A general friction is rising in the air as well, the sound of traffic pressing around and through the neighborhood. The fire rips straight up, and for the first time ever we can hear it roaring over there.

I'm on my hands and knees, staring. Rafferty has collapsed against the fence, his fingers in the links, staring. Witt stands at the end of his bag, hands on his hips, eyes lost in the fire.

"How many runs?" I ask him.

"Sixty-three, man on second. Isn't that what you've got?"

"Yeah, but man on first."

There is a car coming up from Seventh. "You want to quit?"

"You?"

Rafferty runs, returns standing for the single.

The car, the first with its lights out in the new day, passes us for a strike.

"A double and you've tied the record," Rafferty says. "And I'm only six runs down. What a night!"

"I'll quit if you'll quit," I offer. "It's Parley's record."

Witt says, "Jesus, sixty-three runs."

"Man on second," Rafferty adds.

"If he burns that whole damn shed tonight, he's going to be sorry," Witt says. "He won't have anything to burn tomorrow."

"It is tomorrow."

In the clear dawn, an empty bus rattles past, and we take the strike. We take on the Nickel's Market truck, strike two, and we flop out on our bags.

"I say save the record," Witt says, "for when we see Parley again."

"I'm with you," I whisper.

"I'm not sure we'll see Parley again," Rafferty says.

"We won't see a night like this." There's the sound of tires, and we take the third strike lying down. It turns out to be Rudy the Apeman on his motorcycle, headed off to paint stairwells for the State Fairgrounds, and Rafferty lifts off his sleeping bag long enough to give Rudy's back the middle finger. Our game is over.

My mouth tastes funny from being awake so long, but it is undeniably morning. My eyes burn and the hours are burning within me. We can see the ashen edge of the trees, and the birds are going out of control, calling and singing. Mr. Wilkes's fire has shrunk and he has gone inside. There is no more shed. The last of the smoke from the last board trails above us in tatters.

"What a night," Rafferty repeats. "This night."

"We could get that ball before Atom wakes up," I say.

"I could get another cup," Witt says. "Before Ardean gets up."

I smile. "Howard's on third with Slaughter at the plate. And he is one steady hitter."

Witt is up, wrapping his sleeping bag onto his bike. He says, "And Rafferty is under the roof, waiting for a fly ball."

We're going to ride triple on Witt's nutty bike: me on the handlebars, Rafferty on the crossbar. As we get on,

Rafferty says, "Hey, Witt, what about M.M.?"

"Yeah, who is it?"

"Give up?"

"Yeah, we probably give up."

Rafferty's sleeping bag is dragging in the pedals, and he gets off the bike and throws it on the fence. "I'll get it later, okay?"

"Mary Metcalf."

"Mary Metcalf," I say. Mary Metcalf was at Edison Elementary until last February; she wore kilts and went by the nickname Matty. Witt has launched us down the driveway, and we weave onto Derby Street going slower than a walk. Every time Witt's knees come up, Rafferty gets kicked.

"You can't use kids we know," Rafferty says.

"I didn't know her very well," Witt says.

"She wore those weird dresses—"

"Kilts," I interrupt him.

"—and had those red underpants."

"Why'd she move away?"

"What were you doing, watching her on the monkey bars?"

"Too many kids, too much junk."

"What's he talking about?" Witt says, and he leans

into the turn on Concord, bearing down the two-block straightaway. There is a junked car in front of the Oneidas' house, and I know for a certain fact that he's going to try to sideswipe it to give us a scare.

6 air

The Earth's atmosphere is a layer of gases held to the planet by gravity and extending a thousand miles into space. It is composed of 78 percent nitrogen, 21 percent oxygen, and 1 percent argon and other gases. Water vapor and particulate matter are suspended in the atmosphere's lowest layer, the troposphere.

By the end of July, my on-base percentage in Little League is just over four hundred. We decided that a batting average is flawed because it doesn't factor in walks. In batting averages, a walk is not counted as a time at bat. "But that's all it is," Witt argued. "You have to stand there and take four balls. It takes time. You're at bat. And then you get first base. It should count." I was hitting .320, but with the walks, I'm looking real good. Rafferty doesn't care for such discussions, because his coach, Gurber, has not played him yet, one moment. While we talk, he goes off a little ways and swings his bat.

About now, though, Witt comes under new pressure. He talks me into a crazy game of tennis and swings his wicked new tennis racket with a malice that has little to do with sport. It has been building since his sister, Mayreen, locked herself in her room after the incident at Benny's club. She's been in there a week, and it's got everybody nervous. Budd, their father, has always hit what he can't understand, and so there has been a struggle. Now each time Witt smashes the ball, he exhales a sharp "Hup!" as if tennis is a game full of punishments.

It's not really tennis; it's a test. He found three new guitar strings in the garbage behind the pharmacy, still coiled in their paper packages, and laced them through an old warped Jack Kramer racket frame. It looks like a kitchen utensil with those silver strings, and it strikes like a cleaver.

I stand on the rough side of the court and lob the black tennis ball with my racket, and Witt stands like an exterminator, slicing it back at me at rocket speed. Each time he strikes the ball, the racket makes a bimming sound, like someone bumping a piano. The ball is shredding, and finally Witt really swings and the ball knifes right onto the face of the strings, sticking like a piece of cheese. Our experiment is over.

Behind Witt, I can see Rafferty and five other kids playing Fence Tag on the tennis court fence. Roto, Ekins, Keith Gurber, the Starkey twins. They skitter along the ancient wooden four-by-fours that run along the top and the middle of the fence, fingers in the chain link like monkeys. Every so often, someone will fall to the ground and cry for a while and then get up and be it. If you touch the ground, you're it. They all scramble over both sides of the fence, straddling the top, twenty feet off the ground. Occasionally when someone reaches the far end (across the other court where Linda Aikens and Karen Wilkes are playing), the guy who's it will close in, and the victim will try the great leap to the rest room roof. It's something to see. Most kids who attempt the leap simply try a little scream, hit the wall with their feet, and fall to the ground.

Witt and I sit on the lawn while he picks pieces of the ball out of his weapon. "It's going to change the game," he says. "Metal strings. In six months, nylon and catgut are over, you'll see." I already know that Witt doesn't think much of tennis. "The tennis ball is a great thing," he always says. "But tennis is for girls. Any game where you don't get your last ups is not even worth watching."

He hits the racket against his palm a few times to spring loose the last bits of black rubber: *bong, bong, bong.* But there is something in his face that isn't satisfaction; he shakes his head and says, "Mayreen."

A week ago, Atom ran away. Mayreen, his best friend, found him loitering under Benny's clubhouse, leaning against one of the crooked stilts that holds the whole terrible shack eight feet off the ground. The clubhouse itself has no first floor. Four warped two-by-fours hold the cabin aloft just the way Witt designed it. It was going to be a simple eight-foot cube, because Benny and Cling were too lazy to saw any lumber. But when Witt constructed the frame, he made a mistake: he nailed the flat roof on first, and the two bullies had so much fun sitting on top spitting on anything that came down the alley that they told Witt to build the clubhouse up there. The wood was all discard from Shumway Lumber, dragged down the middle of Concord Street by Cling, six boards under each arm. Every two-by-four and plank in the bunch was twisted, warped, knotted, or rotten, which Witt took as a challenge, and he put the structure together like a puzzle. Where one board bowed out, he would counter it with one that twisted the other way. And when he was finished with the second roof, the window, and the half door, he even constructed a four-rung ladder that could be raised and lowered. The clubhouse looked a lot like a tree house—without the tree.

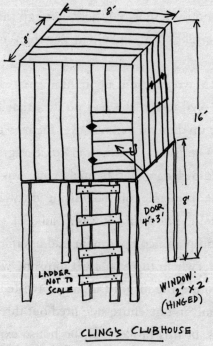

8'

8'

16'

8'

DOOR
4' x 3'

LADDER
NOT TO
SCALE

WINDOW:
2' x 2'
(HINGED)

CLING'S CLUBHOUSE

When I asked Witt why he was doing it, he said it was so those guys would leave us alone for a few weeks. "If those guys are in here," he told me one day last spring as we sat up in the little room, "they can't be down in my yard pulling my hair out and stealing our tennis balls." I felt the shiver each time Witt's hammer struck a nail.

For a week, Benny and Cling spent so much time up there that I kind of missed them. I went through entire days with nothing to avoid, nobody to go the long way around the block for. They had gotten, Witt told me, into sex.

When Mayreen came upon Atom that day leaning against the evil tower, she had no idea that Benny and Cling were up there in a frenzy over the new copy of *Tits Ahoy* that Cling had stolen from some vagrant. It was common knowledge that Benny's club was organized around the principle of looking at dirty magazines. Mayreen didn't know this. It was a bad deal.

The odd plank compartment had assumed a rhythmic and overwhelming wobble. It took one weird, circular tour around the air on those four twisted stilts, and then the nails in one entire side fired out three at a time like bullets, boards broke, and the house exploded and began swinging desperately for the ground. The startled occupants were revealed fully to Mayreen: Benny, his pants knotted around his knees, his hands clutching his privates. Cling still had his pants on, and he stood up and screamed, "Tim-ber!" as he hurled the copy of *Tits Ahoy* into the bright air. By the time that publication floated down, Mayreen had fled down the alley in a beeline toward her room, where she has been for one cruel week. It's been a mess.

Now Cling and Benny slink around the neighborhood, hanging out in Witt's alley quite a bit. Rumor is they want to kill him and nail him to some of the crooked plank remnants of the clubhouse. Benny walks bent over slightly, the way you limp to first after taking an inside pitch in the nuts.

Across from where Witt and I sit today, Linda and Karen tap the ball softly to each other. They're getting better; they can hit it three and sometimes four times in a row before it sails over one of their heads or catches into the net.

I lie back in the grass and tilt my head so I can watch Rafferty moving in the fence. Rafferty is highly skilled in Fence Tag. It's all touch, and he practices a lot at home. He's admitted to me that he plays Furniture Tag even when he's alone. His mother caught him in the living room once, leaping from the coffee table to the sofa, and even though Rafferty was just wearing socks, he was banned from coming upstairs for a week and had to eat his dinner sitting in the hall off the kitchen.

Suddenly Witt jumps up and climbs onto the fence. When he reaches the midpoint four-by-four, he calls, "Two new players; Larry's it." So I rise and pull myself up the huge chain-link fence and start moving along the middle board, like a man on a ledge, herding the seven kids down toward the rest rooms. Once I grab a vine instead of the fence and nearly fall to my death, but other than that, I'm cornering everybody. When one of Roto's friends tries to slip back by edging along the bottom of the fence, I nearly miss him. Roto yells, "Go, Ekins!" and I look and there is this kid trying to midget his way underneath my feet. When he looks up into my face, he says, "No spitting."

Carefully I kneel on the timber and drop into a free hang, swinging my legs a bit too briskly because I kick Ekins in the ear and he drops to the ground and starts crying. I'm sorry for having kicked him, but I say what we say: "You're it, kid." And I hustle along the ledge toward the others. At the end of the fence, we're stacked six deep, and here comes Ekins. Rafferty has gone up, over the top of the fence, hoping to skitter back, when Ekins makes his move. The rest of us await our doom.

Ekins is inching toward us deliberately; no one will escape. Then Witt grabs my shoulder and whispers his plan. It is bizarre, but without thinking I crouch, fingers in the wire, arms straight, so that I lean away from the fence. Witt climbs up above me on the fence and then steps out onto my shoulders. I know what he is thinking. He is not thinking about the game or being it or not being it or falling the twelve feet to the ground; he is thinking, This is something new; this is a move they'll be imitating two summers from now!

Ekins has stopped to witness our acrobatics. In fact, everybody has moved away so as not to be dragged to their deaths with us. Witt, one hand in the fence, is stomping around my shoulders, reaching for balance. Each shift wants to tear my fingers from the fence. Finally he settles, almost sitting on my head.

"Hold on," he says. "Just hold on." I feel a new pressure and realize he is standing up. The roof is only one giant step away from him now. "Okay," he says. "Now, one, two, and the-reee!"

Remarkably I am not hurled to the ground by his springing leap. Witt made it easily. He made it standing up. In fact, he nearly ran off the other side of the rest room. Now, as I rub the deep red creases inside all my knuckles, Witt walks in circles on the rest room roof, gloating.

"How'd he get on the roof?" Rafferty asks from where he sits cocked on the top of the fence.

"Now jump!" Witt says to me. "I'll grab you." I look over at him.

"It only works in movies, Witt."

"Jump!"

I don't want to jump, but I ready myself, as if I could do it. Ekins is coming. He's moving along the fence a little higher than I am to cut off Rafferty's escape.

"One, two . . . "

"Witt," I say.

"I'll catch you."

The Starkey twins, who have both tried this maneuver and battered themselves doing it, are rapt. They cling to the fence just below me for a good view of the suicide.

"Wait a minute," Witt says. "Try this." He retrieves a five-foot two-by-four that lies on the far side of the roof by two old bicycle tires. He jams the plank against the fence crossbar under my feet, and the other edge sits nicely on the roof with four inches to spare. "I'll hold it. Come across." He puts his foot against his end.

I lean back against the chain link and then push and propel myself in two steps right across the narrow bridge onto the roof. I make it. As soon as I set foot onto the shingles, the two-by-four slips and clatters to the ground, nearly knocking the Starkeys' heads off.

"Hey!" Ekins calls. "No fair! You can't do that!"

Witt answers, "Did we touch the ground? What rule did we break? The roof is inbounds."

"You can't use a board."

"Yes we can. Shut up. Catch somebody, or we'll toss a few shingles in your face." Witt tears a wicked triangle out of the roof and holds it up for everyone to see. Then he turns and wings it powerfully out into the sky, where it rises suddenly like a flying saucer and then spins and slices into the grass above the tennis courts. "Go on," Witt says. "Catch somebody. Get Rafferty. He deserves it."

We sit on the roof in the sweet fumes of the two Russian olive trees and the tar shingles and watch the mayhem. Ekins is now way up, one leg over the very top of the fence, and he is side-shifting straight toward Rafferty. Keith Gurber, Roto, and the Starkeys are hunkered against the bottom rung of the fence, as low as they can be without touching the ground.

"I want you to talk to Mayreen," Witt says.

Ekins is closing in on Rafferty. And since Rafferty is an ace in this game, everyone is pretty interested in whatever move he's planning.

"Will you talk to her?"

"Me?"

"Yeah. It's got to be you. She knows you; she doesn't trust Rafferty; and I can't touch it. She thinks I'm going to pound her, which I would really like to do. She's got the whole house crazy. Budd's on the warpath like nothing, and Ardean is crying all the time. You can talk to her."

Witt tears another triangular piece out of the roof and loops it out over Rafferty's head. It lands on the tennis court right in front of Karen Wilkes.

"Please, boys," she says without turning.

"Rafferty, behave," Witt says.

Rafferty doesn't even defend himself; he's lost in concentrating on Ekins. He's perched on the top fence rail like a cowboy, balancing, pretending he isn't twenty feet off the ground.

"Witt, I can't. I don't know what to say."

"It doesn't matter what you say. Just go talk to her. Tell her it's okay if she comes out. Tell her summer is not over. Tell her Benny and Cling were just kidding."

"She's going to believe that."

"She might. You're believable." He looks at Rafferty on the fence. "You're the only believable kid in the neighborhood. Just tell her it was some game."

I'm sorry I walked the plank over to this roof. I do not want to talk to Mayreen. The truth is that I can't explain what Benny and Cling were doing. This neighborhood is crammed with mysteries.

Something new is happening. The Fence Tag changes. Just as Ekins is about to tag Rafferty, he stops and looks straight down. Then here come the Starkeys, Keith Gurber, and Roto, climbing up the fence like prison escapees, scrambling for their lives. All six boys sit astride the top rail of the tall tennis court fence and look down. I can't see what mad dog has scared them all, but then I hear it: Cling's laughter.

"Hey, suckers!" Cling says.

I whisper to Witt to lie flat, and I crawl over to the edge of the rest room roof to see what is going on. Benny and Cling stand against the fence, smoking, blowing the smoke up at the boys. They can't see us, but Witt and I are trapped. "Where's that dipshit Witt?" Benny says, rattling the chain link.

"We don't know," Rafferty says. The six kids look at us.

"That stupid sucker move away or just crawl in a hole?" Benny says, and Cling chokes out his laugh again.

"Why do you want Witt?" Rafferty says.

"Oh, we want to talk to the runt bastard about why he can't build a clubhouse worth a shit."

Just as I move back from the edge, a silver gob of spit sails over my head and down toward Benny and Cling. Witt has spit at them!

There is swearing from below, and I'm guessing that—sight unseen—he was able to strike Cling in the head.

"I've always wanted to do that," he whispers to me. "It was worth it. I'll fight them."

"You piss-ants!" Cling screams, and I see the fence tremble. "You chickenshit piss-ants!" The six boys on top of the fence haven't moved. They look across at us, their faces wide open in fear and surprise. Then they begin to sway.

Benny and Cling are pushing the fence back and forth in a gathering rhythm.

"It was an accident!" Max Starkey tries, but it is no use. The fence continues rocking, back and forth, back and forth. The waves are slower, but wider; the boys have to lean to keep from falling. They must be swaying six feet, back and forth.

"Yee-hah!" Cling calls, enjoying the exercise.

This fence is the biggest thing he's wrecked all week. "Yee-hah!"

The old fence is going to break. Now with each swing, it groans. The boys are flying through the air like apples on a branch. Each time they swing our way, we can see their faces clearly. If I stood up, I could touch them. Roto's face is the only one that shows pleasure; he considers this, like every accident in his life, to be a free ride, and his mouth is open to taste the wind. Ekins looks scared. Keith Gurber has been pantsed twice already this summer by Benny and Cling, and so his face is more resolved. These things are inevitable. Rafferty is holding, practicing a few new positions. But it is the Starkey twins that bother me the most. They look at us helplessly, as if to say, "Thanks very much for having us killed in this way."

Now there is a short, sharp snapping at the end of each deep sway, and that is coupled with a small moaning Ekins has begun. Witt watches the murder calmly, curiously, the way he watches every violent spectacle in this neighborhood, but he is still lying low. I am, too. And then, instead of crashing in an explosion of timber and wire, the old fence leans way out over the tennis courts and lets go. It slumps down, down, down, snaps six or seven times, moans once and stops, three feet from the ground.

Karen Wilkes and Linda Aikens have played tennis through all of this. It is like there is a time zone between all of us and the two girls. I've learned that is the way the world works: boys are being killed, and twenty feet away girls are playing tennis. Karen is now running back to swat a high one, and she runs over Keith Gurber, who has just dismounted the hairiest ride of his life. They both go down in a pile. Keith gets up and runs away. Karen stands up and says to all of us—our friends fleeing to the far corners of the park; Benny and Cling, who stand triumphantly on the fallen fence as if it is an elephant they have slain; and Witt and me, where we cower on the roof—"Grow up! Why don't you all just grow up!" Cling flips his cigarette at her, steps off the fence, and he and Benny swagger off through the swings, past the bandstand, and out of the park.

Linda and Karen take their sweaters and move to the lower court. It is amazing to watch. They just move to the lower court and commence playing their version of tennis. Girls. How do they work? What magical thing surrounds them and enables them to advise Cling to grow up? If I suggested that to him, he'd crush me.

Finally Witt sits up and says, "Did she say grow *up*? Grow up? What for? So we can play tennis?"

I watch how gracefully Linda Aikens moves around that broken tennis court. Then I do one of the weirdest things in this weird summer. When she turns to retrieve the ball, I look at her butt, those smooth, white shorts. How crude is this? I turn my head by force of will and look across the expanse of the Little League park. It is empty, and I can see seven fences, counting the Gibsons'. But there is something in me now that draws me back again to Linda's shorts, and I look again at her backside. Just when you start to feel a little peace of mind, you become a butt-looker. Linda Aikens backs across the jagged cracks as if the court were smooth; she glides left, glides right, runs to the net. She is not going to fall. I look at my dirty sneakers. They've got some miles on them. I am a butt-looker. Oh, please, let it pass.

Twenty-four hours later, riding down Concord Street toward Witt's house, I'm feeling the pressure. The big trees are riding in the wind and several pink Nickel's Market fliers skitter past me along the street and sidewalk. There is a stiff wind in my face and I have to stand up to pedal, but it's more than that: I don't want to talk to

Mayreen. For the first time this summer, I don't want to go to Witt's. The whole neighborhood smells of late lilacs, weed musk, and cut grass. Everything is right except the dusty sky, the wind, and my terrible errand.

Witt is waiting for me in his back lot. I can tell this whole interview means a lot to him, because the first thing he says to me is, "She's in her room." Then, as a gesture of goodwill, he says, "Come here. Look at this." He leads me back through the forest of weeds on a toad path past the burned television set to the old Amana refrigerator sitting near the fence. It still has two notes taped to the door, along with a photo of our second-grade class with Miss Balfour and one of Witt as a baby. Witt taps on the door twice, and two muffled knocks come back. Checking his watch, Witt says to the fridge door, "Four minutes. You all right?"

"No problem." It's Roto's voice.

"He can breathe in there," Witt says.

"That's good to know."

"Yeah, but the experiment is costing me a penny a minute, and I'm not real sure how normal Roto is. It'd be nice to have somebody else. But who else is going to get in the fridge to find out? It's tough to get people into a fridge."

I look at Witt. I want to say, "Not for you, Witt. It's not hard for you." But I turn and walk back toward the house. "She's in her room?"

"Yeah," Witt says. "Let me know how it goes."

As I round the corner toward Mayreen's room, I hear the refrigerator say, "What? What'd you say?"

It feels real funny standing at the corner of the house, calling into the jagged hole, "Mayreen, you in there?" The wind hustles litter across the front yard. "Mayreen?"

"What?"

Okay. I want to move fast, get this over with. I move up to the house and lean into the hole, my elbows on the gritty carpet. The room is a suffocation chamber of dog breath and darkness. At first I can't see anything in the rank humidity, and then my eyes adjust slightly and I can make out a hump on the bed.

"Mayreen?"

"What do you want?"

"Now listen. This is Larry. Those guys . . ."

"I know what those guys were doing."

"Mayreen. Summer's not over. There is no reason not to come out of your room." She doesn't move. "Your friends are asking where you've been."

"Who?"

I don't even know who her friends are; I made that up. But I'm in it now. "That blond girl who isn't as good as you on the tricky bars."

"Shawnee?"

"Yeah, I think so. Shawnee."

The blankets shift, and Mayreen sits up on her bed. "What'd she say?"

"She said she wondered where you've been. She said she hoped you'd come out and play, teach her some tricks on the bars."

She's quiet, so I go on. "If Benny and Cling scared you . . ."

"I hate every boy in the whole world."

"You don't hate me."

Mayreen whispers, "I hate your guts."

I pull back into the windy daylight and the air blows fresh along my throat. I want to say one final thing to Mayreen, but I have no idea what it would be. I walk backward for ten steps, wheeling my arms, but I still feel dizzy, smothered, off center. I want only to go home, hang out in the park, watch batting practice, but I walk past my bicycle and wander along Haslams' fence to the alley, where I sit in the poplars exploding out of Smalls' sheds. I can hear Witt across the weed lot saying something to the fridge.

This is summer; it can't be ruined. You can't ruin summer. There's no spelling test, no cardboard project on the presidents, none of the hefty gloom and pallor of Sunday night. I lean my head back against the rough shed, and something brushes my hair, and I jump, remembering the black widow we found back here last summer. But this isn't a spider. It's something hanging in the branches, and when I poke it and take hold, it becomes Mayreen's violin, the brown body. I tug the strings, and the neck of the instrument follows me into the daylight.

Back in the dank space of Mayreen's room, I flop the violin components out onto her littered floor and I say, "We can fix this for you." The rest just follows, the way the Gettysburg Address fell out of my mouth last February in front of our class. "Mayreen," I say. "Mayreen. It's okay. It's okay to come outside. Summer is not over. There is still a ton of stuff to do."

That's it. I extract myself from the hole in the corner of the house as if I am taking a bow, and I stand and brush the lint off my arms for a moment. I spit. I feel better. I did what I could. I grab one of the passing pink sheets for the Nickel's Market butcher specials and crumple it in my hand and throw it onto the roof. When it floats down, I make the catch. Oh, it feels good to be outside.

However, in the back lot, things look bad. Benny and Cling have finally caught up with Witt. Actually all I can see is their heads above the blowing weeds. They are looking down. I imagine they have clobbered Witt fully and now are taking turns kicking him.

Before thinking, I yell, "Hey! What's going on?" But when I arrive at the old refrigerator through the jungle trail, it is different than I supposed.

"Witt killed his brother," Benny explains.

The fridge door is yawning open, releasing a stale odor too concentrated to be dispersed by this wind, and Roto is limp on the ground with Witt kneeling above him. Roto is a light green, the color of celery. In fact, he smells like rotten celery.

"Seventeen minutes," Witt says to me.

"Yeah, well, you're a weird kid, Witt," Cling says, "to kill your little brother."

"We were pissed at you because of the monkeyshit job you did on the clubhouse, but, hell, we're not going to beat you up in front of your dead brother."

The two guys move back through the weeds and into

the alley. "We'll see you around," Benny calls. "Sorry about your brother."

"Yeah," Cling adds from the distance. "I did a lot of shit, but I never killed my brother!"

Witt stands up and closes the fridge door. Then he opens it again. Then he closes it. Then he opens it and runs his fingers along the rubber door liner. "That's quite a seal they put in these things."

Roto is still sprawled green beneath us.

"Seventeen minutes," Witt says. "Have you got a quarter? Lend me a quarter. Don't worry, I'll write it in the book."

I hand Witt my quarter. He kneels again and deposits it in Roto's open palm. I am amazed to see the fingers close around it. Witt sees my surprise and says, "Yeah, it was only seventeen minutes, but what the heck, I'll give him a bonus this time." I see Roto's open mouth close and then open again.

He moves his head to the side. He's either less green now or a different shade of green. Maybe it's yellow. "Let's go before he throws up," Witt says, pushing me back toward the house.

I want away from here. I want to mount my bike and fly with the wind down to the park where kids will be just playing games. I throw my leg over the bike. Witt comes up and puts his hands on the handlebars. "Is she coming out?"

"We have to fix her violin. That's all I know."

He sits in the wheelbarrow without a wheel, like a man in a recliner, and I leave him there, and I rise on one pedal and drift around the house. I rush the street on my bike and rise into the sweet wind, turning with it in a fast sweep down Concord. I race a dust devil that is spinning old vocabulary tests and dirt across the schoolyard, when I hear my name in the wind. Coasting, I stand on the pedals and turn in time to see Mayreen wave at me from the front yard. I can see the wind pulling at one end of her blanket and Atom at the other, like two creatures trying to fold a flag.

The toughest part of the Gettysburg Address is the hump around the word *consecrate*, which is in there twice. I say the word now and feel it torn from my mouth by the wind. Old Miss Talbot, she wasn't so bad. The wind fills my shirt for a moment, but then I'm flying faster than the air; I outrace fleets of pink paper and cut through the narrow gate at the park without slowing down. I do it fast, knowing that if I catch a handlebar on the gate, I'll be upside down and bleeding. Sometimes it is so simple to love my life. Down on the Little League diamond, I can see Rafferty's team being driven from the field by the dust storm. A few kids chase their caps in the brown air. Ekins and the Starkey twins are horsing around on the rest room roof, throwing torn shingles high into the crazy wind and watching them rise and dive.

But what stops me in this mad weather, what makes me slow and lean a handlebar against the side of the old bandstand, is not all of these activities, nor the blasting summer whirlwind, the grit hitting my face, nor the dusky haze hovering over the park, but the two girls playing tennis. I see Linda and Karen, their hair winging away from their heads, playing tennis in this warm wind, and I stop to watch them.

It stuns me. My eyes almost water against the air as I watch Karen and Linda struggle against the elements. I will never understand girls, but I see now that they are braver than I thought. They run and bat the ball into the unreliable sky, even though they must know, as I do now, that the air is full of things and anything could happen.

part three

AUGUST

7 the great wheels of time

No branch of science has fostered more theories than the study of time and its relationship to the physical world. Mankind used the cycles of nature to first measure time and to coordinate societal functions. All motion is somehow linked to the entity we call time, and this remains the deepest mystery in scientific inquiry.

Summer passes strangely. Because we sleep out so often, the days merge and flow. Some days we lounge in the park, taking sun, not even moving when the sprinklers snap over us, dreaming until late afternoon, when kids show up in their uniforms for the Little League game. Other days are frantic, jammed with two things at once, a game of Cup Baseball and chemistry experiments, Witt taking time out to pound his sister or torment the dog. Some afternoons I'm so run with fatigue that I don't know what day it is. "Every day is Saturday" is Witt's motto. And I lose track of our place in all of it, and I sit against the home-run fence in the park feeling like the oldest person in the neighborhood.

Nights we lie under thirty billion sizzling stars, and Witt tries to explain how the sky works: 1) stars are out all day, too, 2) it takes years for the starlight to get here, 3) to see certain stars you look near them, not at them, 4) the Big Dipper, 5) the North Star, 6) the Milky Way, 7) stars are in different places as August arrives. We don't get it. I only know summer is the dearest thing there is, that I can play ball with my two friends until the world goes purple and two planets come out by the moon.

The second day of August, after Coach Robbins lets us go from Little League practice, I slide my mitt on my handlebars and cruise Concord like a king. I arrive just in time, gliding softly up Witt's old driveway and steering my bicycle around the corner of the house as Witt is wiping his chin. I've been spared. He's finished vomiting.

"It was a test," he shrugs, his face white. He's still clutching the stalk of a huge green alfalfalike weed. He's eaten half of it, and his teeth marks cut a crescent in the end. The weed grows everywhere in the neighborhood and can reach six feet tall in a sunny spot if it leans against a fence. Witt's yard is choked with it. "It's terrible," he says, and flings the tattered weed into the geothermal pit. "Don't eat it. It starts out okay, but it turns on you. It's fundamentally terrible. Just don't."

"Thanks, Witt. I won't."

"You can eat these, though." He quickly plucks one of the flat, spreading weeds from the ground. We call them thornos because they look just like the flowering thorn weed that can flatten a bike tire in a minute. He holds it up like a green lace handkerchief and nibbles the edge. "They're a little bitter, but they won't make you sick."

"None for me," I say, leaning on my bicycle. "I wouldn't care for any right now."

By the time Witt retrieves his bike from the side yard where Mayreen and two of her friends have it upside down, cranking the sprocket pretending to make ice cream, his color has returned.

He leads me out onto Concord and then stands on the pedals saying "Lumber!" the way soldiers call "Charge!" in westerns, and we race five blocks down Nevada Avenue to the lumberyard.

I already know that we're going to haul some two-by-fours back to Witt's. Witt claims to have figured out the very secret of time. He is going to build a Time Tower. I don't care. As long as we can ride our bikes, taste this wind, rush this air, I don't care.

The discard pile outside the fence of the lumberyard is low, but there are a few twisted two-by-fours lying in the wet grass. Witt places one across his handlebars, I do the same, and we start back, wobbling. It's like flying an airplane, balancing the crooked eight-foot studs across our handlebars, trying not to crash into parked cars or let the boards pinch our fingers off.

When we swoop back onto Concord, there's Rafferty on Witt's front porch, waiting for us. "That's no good," Raff says as we unload the two planks. "One at a time? Who're you kidding?"

So he rides double with Witt back to the lumberyard. I can hear them behind me. Witt is telling Rafferty about eating weeds: "I think if you stuck to it, maybe starting with younger plants, you could eat the stuff. Why should there be things you can't eat?"

At the lumberyard, Witt stacks four of the long boards across his handlebars and then Rafferty sits on top of all of them to hold them down.

"No problem!" he says, though Witt is having a little trouble keeping the bike from falling over. "Four at once! Roll the wagons!"

They can't roll at all, and finally I put down my one board and my bike. I steady Witt and Rafferty, running to give them the push to start them down Nevada.

"We're the Wright brothers!" Rafferty cries. He's having fun. "We're going up Bowman's alley. Come on, Larry, where are you?"

I'm right behind them, watching them totter down the street. It really does look like they might take off. The four warped timbers splay wickedly to each side, and the whole contraption looks like a quadruple-winged airplane.

When they enter Bowman's alley, I'm still right on their tail. Witt is having a ball. His legs kick wildly to both sides and he is calling "Whoa, big fella" and making deep, humming, airplane noises. His head jumps right and then left to see around Raff. The alley is narrow, and it's all a lot like cruising an airplane in a canyon.

We almost make it.

Witt guides them all the way through the alley, past the bad spot where the willows grow out of Ketchums' sheds, but when he crosses Western and dips into his alley, they hit an old car door lying hidden in the weeds. The sharp bump jangles Raff up off the load, and the two-by-fours fan out like spokes. One catches Haslams' fence. Rafferty's hands are pinched in the scissors of the boards, and he is thrown headfirst into the gravel. When he goes down, I see the other end of the plank come up and swipe Witt in the neck, taking him off the bicycle like a scythe.

I brake hard, sending my single two-by-four off the front, where it is able to trip my wheel, jam the bike, and send me over the handlebars.

In the past four years I've flown from my bike like this seven times now, losing physical contact with it and leaving it behind. Seven, I think as I'm in the air. These flying accidents happen so fast I can never remember how I end up sitting in the weeds. I must hit and roll or slide, bounce a little, but I'm guessing. Time collapses, and I fall through.

Witt is up first, examining his lumber. By the time he's found all the boards, Rafferty is already fifty yards down the alley. "Hey! Rafferty! Don't go! That was great! Nothing's broken!"

Witt and I alone deliver twelve two-by-fours total to Witt's backyard that afternoon. Later he sits on the menacing stack of lumber and pulls a piece of paper from his back pocket.

"There," I say. "Now let's play ball."

"Let's not play ball," he says. "Let's do this." He unfolds the paper and shows me this drawing:

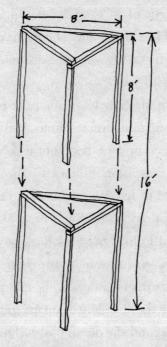

"You know what this is?"

"Let's go find Rafferty and you can tell him you're sorry, and we can get in a little Over the Line."

"Look it over. Really. What is it?"

"Witt," I say. I can tell he's opening a new chapter in a serious project, and I'm not sure I want to be part of it. "We flew the boards down here. Rafferty had his ass pinched off. I personally have been over my handlebars. Let's play ball. Let's just go down to the park and watch the minor league play." I stand above him in the first sad, blond light of late afternoon. The day is closing down.

"Wrong," he says, waving the document at me. "This is a Time Tower."

As if to underline his pronouncement, there is a whine that suddenly ceases and then rises again. It sounds like a cat under a boot, but it is Mayreen over by the scorched television cabinet in the weeds, leaning against the old fridge. We can just see her head, playing her newly repaired violin. She's been playing every day since Witt and I glued the neck back on the thing using homemade epoxy: cornstarch, turpentine, and fingernail polish. "Harder than diamonds," he told me. She actually stores it now in the abandoned Amana fridge, never taking it in the house, and she doesn't play "Three Blind Mice" at all, but a rocky medley of tunes of her own devising. She plays with a steely determination. Mostly it sounds like a mad person moaning in the bushes. But she's happy.

Witt stands stock still, looking at Mayreen's blissful face as the sounds wash over us. She's out of her room, but there are some obvious drawbacks to that. "Let's go to the park," he says, all business, folding the plans for his Time Tower into his pocket.

The park is empty; we're way early for the minor league game. Rafferty's bicycle is leaning against the backstop, and we find him flopped out on the bleachers, practicing his new deep-tanning technique: stretching. He drapes himself over one of the planks like a rug on a clothesline.

"Stretches the skin," he groans up at us. "Better tan. Although that is not the sun." He points upside down to the west, his palm at the sky. "It's just light. The sun has moved on, right, Witt?"

"Real good, Rafferty," I say. "We believe you. Now, about that dime you owe me."

"I can't hear you."

I walk around and stand face to upside-down face with him. "It's in the book. Ten cents." I hold out my hand. "I guess I could accept a little can of mandarin oranges." Even upside-down he looks desperate, and I know I'll have my way again. Witt has draped Raff's shirt over his head; he has freckles and hates this sun business. Even so, I can sense he's frowning.

This time, when Rafferty returns, he has no oranges. He hands me a loaf of bread.

"What's this?"

Rafferty looks at Witt. "What do you mean," he says. "It's bread. I can't take any more oranges; there are only two cans left."

I look at the bread, holding it up and hefting it in my hand like a swollen baseball. "Bread," I say. "What do I want with bread? I can eat bread at my house."

Witt is crossing out the debt in the book.

"Wait a minute!" I point at him. "Don't cross that out. I don't accept this!"

"Too late," Witt says. "It's done. Besides, it's more than an even trade."

There is something wrong. I am in the baseball park holding a loaf of bread. I stand up on the top row of those bleachers beside my friends, and I extract the bread from its wrapper and throw each slice out above the baseball diamond, where it spins and sails like a small white Frisbee, landing softly by second base. Bread can really fly. Rafferty laughs while Witt sits watching, giving me the hard stare.

"Well," I say, "I didn't want a loaf of bread, particularly." I keep throwing, and for a moment the air is full of bread. But even as I'm tossing each slice, I think: some things are not supposed to fly, even for a minute.

* * *

After dinner that night, I meet my pals again in the park, and I am feeling like my old self. Rafferty's little brother is pitching a no-hitter against the Hornets, and right in the middle of the baseball fury, looking like a lamb gone through a lawn mower, is all that bread. In the action, some has been tracked halfway to third, and some has been scattered into shallow center. Mrs. Rafferty sits in row one, her arms folded in her way, watching her son pitch. Beside her is Rudy the Caveman, cheering Little Markie and calling some of the other kids names, mainly "chicken" and "chick-chick chicken." Rafferty taps me and points at his pocket. I can see his other hand in there giving Rudy the Caveman the finger. I've never seen this before, flipping off someone from the pocket, but I'm counting it, because we're at close range. It feels dangerous.

When we pass Mrs. Rafferty as we climb up, I say, "Good evening, Mrs. Rafferty." She does not say, "Hello, Lawrence." Does she know? Can she tell it's her bread? My heart feels like a nuclear accident. I sit trying to watch without looking at the torn bread, which beams at me like radioactive particles.

Then there is a yell as the game ends and all of Little

Markie's teammates throw their gloves into the air. Everyone drifts away from the park, and the concession stand is boarded up, and it really starts to get dark, and I feel like the last person left in the world.

Rafferty has walked home behind his mother and Rudy and Little Markie to get his sleeping bag. Witt has dropped off the top of the bleachers to the ground and said, "See you later," and left. I stay as long as I can, hoping things will somehow become normal again, but the bread is magnified in the dark, so finally I slip down the bleachers and walk my bike home to get my sleeping bag.

When I drift into his backyard, Witt's nailed the first level of the tower together, six wicked two-by-fours in a triangle on stilts, and the structure is as straight as the ruined lumber will allow. Before Witt can really crank into his lesson on the Time Tower, Rafferty, proud, shows us his two fingers bruised blue from being crimped royally in the bicycle-lumber crash, but Witt isn't interested in blue digits. He knows about bruises, how they work. We've seen them on his chest, arms, for years.

Then he reaches into his pockets and says, "Boys, I've got something to show you."

He lays out seven little brass wheels on the back of his

baseball notebook and says, "Here it is."

Raff and I study the display. The bright disks reflect the early evening light beautifully. Neither of us is going to bite and ask him what they are, but we both nod. Rafferty goes so far as to select one of the tiny cogs. He examines it. Against his blue fingers, it looks really pretty. "I've been thinking about time," Witt says, and then I can recognize the pieces as the wheels from a watch. "It's relatively simple."

"That's what I was thinking," Rafferty says, giving Witt back the shiny disk.

"You see how it works?"

I sit down, glad to find one of Atom's blackened tennis balls so I'll have something to play with while we receive this lecture.

"Yeah, we see," Rafferty says. "Three o'clock: practice. Five-thirty: game time. Seven-thirty: dinner. Eight o'clock: meet you and Larry so you can torture us with this crap."

"It all turns," Witt goes on. "You should see the way these things work together." He indicates the wheels. "You see how they're all different sizes." He's cruising. "Now what else turns?"

Rafferty sits down. He's done his best, and he lies

back in the weeds fully and puts his arm over his eyes. I toss the ball up and try to catch it behind my back. We're waiting for our friend Witt to return to us; sometimes a catch can get his attention. "Let's eat weeds," Raff says. "I understood that. Let's just eat a few of these weeds."

Witt stands patiently before us. He's going to give his students one more chance. "Now what else is round?"

"A tennis ball?" I say.

"Now that's five points for sure," says Raff.

"A tennis ball! A tennis ball!" Witt has lost it. He yells, "The Earth? Could the Earth be round? A tennis ball!" He grabs the tennis ball from me before I can try another behind-the-back toss, and says, "The Earth is a tennis ball!"

"I knew it was the Earth," Rafferty says. "Who gets the five points? Is there a bonus question?"

In his anger, Witt flips his bicycle upside down. He sets it before us as if he is now going to make ice cream the way the little kids pretend.

"Watch, you guys, please." And then he whispers, "Nobody knows this. Nobody. Watch." Then he spits it all out, and between me and Rafferty, about 20 percent is received. He explains that the rear tire is the Earth. He sticks a little thorn in the surface of the tread and slowly rotates the tire. I think we are supposed to be the thorn on the turning tire. We're supposed to see how far we went around the Earth. Now he jams the tennis ball in the spokes beneath the thorn. I don't know who the tennis ball is supposed to be. He rotates the wheel once and says, "For five points: who went the farthest?"

"How long do we get to answer?" Rafferty says.

The short story—in which no one gets the five points—is that the thorn went farther. Time, according to Witt, is tied up in all of this. After turning the tire about seventy times, he takes the thorn and shinnies up the unfinished Time Tower and sticks it in the top cross beam. We can't see it. He throws the tennis ball into the geothermal pit, which is a mistake because Atom the retrieverdog wasn't fully asleep, and he leaps over Rafferty after it and disappears.

"The point is," Witt tells us, speaking real slowly, "the *higher* you are, the *farther* you travel each day, and the *older* you get—faster."

"Makes sense to me," Rafferty says, getting up. "That's why older kids are taller than we are. And Witt. I want you to know that when they put you away, I'm going to visit so you'll have somebody to play catch with." Rafferty shakes his torn sleeping bag and lays it out regally on a bed of springy green weeds. He lies down upon it and crosses his ankles. "There's no reason a crazy person can't keep a good throwing arm."

. We finally get Witt to play a little Pop Up, where you lie on your back and you have to throw the ball up ten feet into the dark and catch it lying in the same place. The trick is not to let the ball drift toward your feet. Then Rafferty is asleep and then Witt, his mouth open, each breath a little huff in the murky night. I float for a while and then a long while, but I can't drop off. The crickets are in their second shift, ripping the edge of everything, a sound track laid down for the buzzing stars. I know what it is, and finally I sit up and extract myself from my trusty old flannel sleeping bag with its pattern of bears and ducks.

I move down the streets at a jog, avoiding the bright spills of the street lamps. It is creepy out here, everything shut up, the houses sunken in the dark, the whole world gone somewhere else. It is as if there is a famine. The park is black. It is late late. The tennis court lights have been out for hours and there is no moon, only the bright crumbs of stars thrown around the sky. I am as alone as I ever have been, and the aloneness feels like a pressure on my heart, a test that wants to show me who I am. I find the fence with my hands and jump over onto the playing field. It seems huge in the dark and I walk in circles amid the glowing bits of bread, expecting to bump into something. I've become nocturnal; that's the word Miss Miller would use from the Vocabulary Cabinet. As soon as I think of the word, I know that it's true and I feel bad for my parents. They hardly know me. They don't know I'm nocturnal. They don't know they've raised a son who is nocturnal. And that he is a butt-looker. Why, oh why, would I look at Linda Aikens's butt? For ten days I've been a nocturnal butt-looker, and it is not wearing off. What a condition, I think as I kneel and pick up a crust of bread. This summer is being hard on me. On my hands and knees I work toward shortstop, pinching crumbs from the grass and stuffing them into my pocket. Crawling like that, it takes me an hour to get what I can, walk back to Witt's, and fall asleep in the weeds with my friends.

A couple days later, Rafferty goes on vacation with his mother and brother to Durango, Colorado, where they have relatives. If he's gone long, he could miss a lot. Mrs. Rafferty asked me to water their yard while they are away. I stood inside her screen door and watched for a sign that she knew I was the nasty thief who had emptied her food supply and eaten all the mandarin oranges, but I could not read her beautiful face or her voice, and I was sure she could read mine, so I did not stay very long.

Now I water their yard twice a day, once for the front and once for the back, such as it is, just to keep the dust down. But it's no good being in a friend's yard when he's away. I play Little League. The shortstop, Wedgie Stewart, and I turn three double plays in one game. I hit my sixth home run, a pop-up really, but the wind holds it long enough for it to clear the right-center fence. Our team, the Blue Hats, has the title nearly clinched, and Mr. Robbins gives the younger kids more time in batting practice. Max Starkey refuses to pay Cling his extortion nickel one day down near the swings and gets killed. I wasn't there, but that's the way my brother Eddie describes it: "He got killed." Eddie doesn't have the good sense to run home when trouble starts; he watches everything in the neighborhood. Sometimes I think he's worse than I am.

I don't see much of Witt for a while. He doesn't come to our games, and when I cruise his yard, he's gone. I feel the summer lose a stitch. Karen Wilkes and Linda Aikens still play tennis every day. They're not really getting any better. At night now, I sleep down in the basement with my brother Eddie, and it is strange to be inside all night.

The sleep-out record is kaput. In our room it's quiet, and I sleep later than I ever have. At bedtime, Eddie and I play Name That Tune by knocking on the wall until Mom yells for us to stop. Then we play it scratching on the sheet. We play until we fight; he guesses my song as "A-wimba-way," and I tell him no such song. As he slaps at me, I taunt him with "It's 'The Lion Sleeps Tonight,' you dummy." When Mom calls down the second time, we roll apart to sleep. After a while I can hear Eddie scratching the sheet and humming his tune, practicing for tomorrow night.

I'm watering the front lawn when the Raffertys return from their vacation. Actually, I'm hosing the ants off the front sidewalk and having a pretty absent time, but it looks good. Mrs. Rafferty thanks me and pays me a dollar and a quarter, which means five days have gone by. I watch my old nearsighted pal Rafferty help unload the car. Five days. The summer is passing just like that.

That afternoon, Rafferty and I prowl for Witt. His backyard is rife with the pungency of inedible weeds, and above it all, above the litter and the trenches and the rusting debris, stands the Time Tower. Witt has completed the second shelf, and the whole thing looms and leans sixteen feet into the sky. It is a magnificent and gruesome piece of work, the tallest thing anybody's built in this neighborhood since Mr. Haslam put up his basketball backboard. Raff goes to one of the uprights and gives it a shake. The whole structure gyrates.

"I was wrong about the triangles," Witt's voice comes from deep in the weed jungle. He whacks his way toward us with his metal-stringed tennis racket. In his other hand is the white cloth marble bag bulging with his bottle-cap men. "It's shaky as hell."

"It takes a big man to admit his failure," Rafferty says, giving the tower a good wobble.

"We can't sleep out up there," Witt says. "I'm not even going to finish the platform."

"No, we might as well not sleep up there," Rafferty says. He could topple the whole thing with a good push.

"You guys want to play a little Bottle-cap Baseball?" Witt asks.

"Why were we going to sleep up there?"

"It's a Time Tower, Rafferty. We'd be staying at a higher elevation than anybody in the neighborhood. We'd be able to get older than other kids. You know what elevation is, don't you, Raff?"

"You've got this all figured out, haven't you, Larry?"

Rafferty says to me.

"Oh, sure," I say. "A Time Tower. The higher the older."

"Is that why all the kids around here sleep in the basements?"

"Yep."

"And every time you climb a tree, you get older?" Rafferty, like any kid, has a high tolerance for things he doesn't know, but here he gives Witt a real long look as if to say, "And what else do they do on your home planet?" Then he says to me, "He's your friend."

Rafferty sits beneath the Time Tower. He picks one of his bottle-cap men from the mound of dirt beside him and holds it up to show us. It's an Orange Crush cap, a guy Raff uses as a pinch hitter. Raff walks the bottle cap along the back of his hand and then flips him up and over into the geothermal pit.

"Ahhhhhhh!" He makes a little scream. I can see in his very posture that Rafferty is full of a sharp sorrow for the way he has chosen his friends this summer.

Witt still stands, hands on his hips, scanning his tower. It may be shaky; it may be useless; but Witt is proud of it. It takes Rafferty a minute to remember the dollar and a quarter that I have in my pocket and suggest a trip to the pharmacy, all expenses paid. Walking down there, Raff looks back at the skeletal frame of the Time Tower. "Falling off that thing would stop time," he says. "Is that what you were after, Witt?"

I think it all over that night after dinner. I am tying my sleeping bag onto my back fender when my mother calls Eddie into the house: bedtime. He will go downstairs and sleep in our room. No wonder he's my little brother. No wonder he's not getting as old as I am. In the deep brown twilight, I stand on the lawn and look up at the pearly full moon. I can feel it following the world. I pat the sleeping bag and mount up. "Behave," my mother says as I start to pedal. I sense that soon I will be as old as she is. I call back too loudly, "I will, Mom! I will!"

Witt and Rafferty have already started Car Baseball in Witt's front yard. I hear Raff say that he's running on me and it's going to be a triple home run.

"You can't run on bicycles," Witt says, sitting on his bag, watching for cars.

"All I want," Rafferty says to me as I arrive and unroll my bag, "all I want in my whole life, even if it is one hundred and ninety years long, all I want is one summer— no, one week—when I make up the rules, when I act like a madman and I still get to make up all the rules." Rafferty ignores a passing truck, taking the strike, while Witt nabs a single. "Larry, you should see this kid. He just ate one of Haslams' roses. He wants me to try one."

"Sit down, Rafferty," Witt says quietly. "Save it. You can't run on bicycles."

"Unless they have a light," Rafferty comes back.

"Unless they have a light."

"These rules!" Raff throws his arms above his head. "Larry, go eat a rose."

"Easy, Raff, easy."

"Oh, easy? Sure, no problem. I'll go back and sleep on the Time Tower for a while. That should make me older and wiser." And he laughs like a maniac, like Dr. Demento and his Pig-Men, while Witt alertly runs for another single on a grocery van that's turned the short corner. When he slides in, he says to us, "Strike two, you bozos."

We sit expectantly on our sleeping bags for a while, hoping to play more Car Baseball, but it's dead. Too quiet. No cars. Not even Old Man Wilkes in his evil Plymouth. With the score 3 to 1 to 1, we quit and drag our stuff into the backyard. On the way, Rafferty points at the tower and says, "Witt. You want to do something interesting?"

"I am doing something interesting."

"No. Forget this time thing. Teach me how to fly. Figure that out. You could do it; teach me how to fly." Rafferty's serious.

Witt throws his ragged bedroll on the weeds.

"Come on. Let's fly. What is it, air? Air. You could do that, Witt."

"It is air. You can't fly."

"Why?"

Witt steps up behind Rafferty and nudges him so he falls softly, but completely, into a hole. He's down there tangled in his sleeping bag, looking up. "You can't fly. You can rest there in the dirt. If you want to get up, I'll be glad to try to teach you how to walk."

"It's all right, Rafferty," I say. But he reclines there, hissing lowly.

Ten minutes later, Rafferty has subsided. He reclines in the hole like a man watching television. He is squinting at the features in the moon as we play One Thousand, the psychic game where you try to guess the number. No one's been within three hundred.

"I'm sending," I say. Around us the crickets raise thick static.

After a moment, Witt says, "Could you send just a bit

harder? Don't let your mind wander."

"Five hundred fifty-five," Rafferty says. "I got it, right?"

"I'm not through sending."

"Start again; Rafferty wrecked it."

"Five fifty-five," Rafferty says.

"It was eight hundred and one. You send, Witt."

"I had the one part," Witt says.

"Are you sure you didn't think five fifty-five?" Raff says.

"I'm sure," I say. "Witt, are you sending?"

"Okay. Just a minute. Clear your minds."

"No problem."

"Here it comes."

I lean back in the dark and watch the moon roll across the top beam of the Time Tower. I'm trying to think about the numbers, and finally I get a small fix on one twenty-three, but it shakes and goes away and all I can think of is Parley. Parley's gone. Parley has gone away. Each year the older kids in the neighborhood disappear. Each year there are more younger kids in the park. Where is everybody going? The neighborhood, gripped as it is in weeds and decay, is changing. Above us the moon looks like a spotlight on a guard tower and blasts

Witt's yard with harsh light, cutting our faces in half, sharpening every leaf blade.

"I'm getting it!" Rafferty says. "I'm getting it!" He holds both hands to his temples. "I am receiving." He sits up. "Okay. Okay. I got it: Five . . . fifty . . . five! Right? I got it."

Witt opens his eyes from his sending trance. He rolls over. "Let's go to sleep," he says. "Let's just go to sleep." The moon slides to the edge of the tower; it looks ready to roll off.

"What was the number?"

"Go to sleep, you guys."

So it's quiet for a moment, quiet with the crickets roaring into outer space, and then Rafferty says, "Say, do you ever think we're just mirrors of another world out there? That there are these three kids sleeping out. . . ."

"Don't start, Raff," Witt says. "Don't even start with the mirror world speech. Go to sleep. If there is a mirror world, there's a kid up there who is a royal pain in his mirror world's ass. Just go to sleep."

Now Witt makes a big huff about readjusting all the rips in his sleeping bag, patting them, moving them all back over his legs, settling them, and then lying down with a disgusted exhalation. He closes his eyes, but too firmly, and after ten seconds I see him open them again. He's squinting at the Time Tower.

"You really think it's elevation, Witt?"

"Oh, yeah," he says. "It's elevation. That's the way the world ages."

"Why don't you guys just sleep on the house?" Rafferty blurts. He's joking, but Witt sits up.

"What?"

"On the distant mirror planet, some kid is sleeping on the roof, seeing if he gets older."

"Cool it, Rafferty." I want to let this pass, to let the moon reach across the alley and drop behind Smalls' sheds, ending the murderous light so we can sleep until tomorrow. But Witt is already up. With a wild, loopy windup, looking like the mad cowboy, Witt swings his sleeping bag around and throws it onto the house. Watching him do it, I know I'm going up there, too. My policy this summer is to join him. If I had to think about it each time, I'd miss everything. But for the first time I wonder if it is a good policy, if this is something I should do.

The roof is steeper than it looks from below. And smaller. From up here Witt's yard looks like a blurred photograph in a bad newpaper, some mistake. I can't see Rafferty at all; then his head pokes out of his ditch and catches light.

"How is it?" he calls. "You feel older?"

"It's okay," I reply, quieter than I intended.

To my right Witt is fussing around, and finally he turns to me and says, "Do this." He has arranged his sleeping bag from the crest of the roof down the forty-degree slope so that his feet reach the standpipe below him. I do the same and realize this is going to be like trying to sleep while leaning against a wall.

"I'm going to sleep in this hole," Rafferty calls. "I want to be a kid forever."

Witt answers, "You've got a chance, Raff. You've got a real good shot at it." Then he turns to me. "If you feel yourself slipping, just grab the pipe." He lies back, his hand behind his head like the executive vice president of the universe. "We're going to travel hundreds of miles farther than Raff by morning."

I watch his face in the bright, flat moonlight, trying to figure out if I should be scared. He wears that high grin I always see when he's on the edge of something. We're laid out on the roof in the moonlight like sunbathers. Witt squirms sideways and takes the watch parts out of his pockets and holds them in his hands like coins. He spreads the shiny wheels in his palm and sorts them with a finger. "They'd never make money this beautiful," he says. He holds one up in front of the moon. There is another one so tiny that he can hold it on a fingertip.

I feel myself slipping all night long. In periodic fits of waking, I grab the crest of the roof six or seven times. Maybe twenty. I don't know. The roof is hard and tries to throw me off. Then the moon is down and I'm on my side, trying to cover myself without moving in the fresh cold air.

I wake and sleep and wake and sleep in the chill. The cold has little teeth in my bones now. I lie on my side, my head against the roof, and listen to the house measure time, ticking strangely at intervals I cannot guess. I don't want to get older, out of school, out of my parents' home, out in the world. My parents will be old and then die, and then I will be out there, old and alone, standing in the old park alone, no neighborhood crawling with kids in the dark night. I can feel the cold house riding hard through the world, the air above me rising to the nothingness of space, dark cold black cold, my brothers in other cities, no baseball, no dinnertime, no lights on in the window as I run across the park for home. No bushel of apples inside the garage door in the early fall, no clean sweatshirts on the bed, no bed at all, just this slanted roof, freezing me, my feet swollen in the terrifying gray night from sleeping at a hard angle while the Earth turns.

I open my crusted eyes. Witt is sitting beneath me, straddling his standpipe in the bare dawn. "Hey," I whisper. "Let's get down."

"I can feel it," Witt says. He's electric. "I can feel it. I can feel time passing." He stretches his arms out cautiously as if he is letting go the reins of this large rocking horse, his house, and he opens and clenches his hands again and again. "I can feel it all around us." His eyes are closed.

I try to sit up, but I am chilled thoroughly and my neck is stiff. I roll over and slide down until I too am straddling a pipe on the roof. I don't want to let go of the pipe, but I reach out one arm and open my hand. There is a small breeze, the fresh, wet, summer dawn rising along the shingles around us. It smells wonderful, of clover and weeds and rust and faintly of water leaving warm cement.

"Can you feel it?" Witt asks.

Behind him, I can see the outline of old Edison

Elementary developing in the grainy light. I can hear an airplane dragging itself across the top of the sky. My skull hums with fatigue.

Witt was right. Time is passing. I can feel the whole night burning in the base of my brain, behind my eyes. It is the ache of time. Time is passing through my head like friction tape. This is it, I think: time is passing; it makes me dizzy. "Yeah," I say to Witt. "I can feel it going through us right now." I grab the pipe with both hands. "Can we get down?"

"Look at him. He looks like a baby." Witt points down at Rafferty who, cradled in his nest, does look like a baby for the moment before my eyes blur. I am staring at him when my eyes melt over for the first time, and my head rolls back in a waving, hot clamp. I can barely hold on to the house; it undulates beneath me. It rocks under me like a swollen raft. It floats, heaving softly in the thick air. I lie back and feel the warm rolling house; I can't open my eyes.

"What's the matter?" Witt asks, and I can barely feel him touch my shoulder. I'm trying to hold on to the pipe, but the house is now clearly turning out from underneath me, sloughing me off easily, as I wheel around the pipe until my head is down here, Witt reaching for me, my hands unable to make a fist, each finger pulling softly off the pipe like old soft rubber, and as the last thing: Witt's hands on my shoulder turning me back one little bit—as the roof edge grabs my neck—so that when I drop, I don't hit my head.

How many times do we get to fall? How many of these passages through the air do I get? My body slugs into the ground. I'm immediately too hot to breathe, and I try to stand up, and I really fall now, right on Rafferty. When I slid off the roof, Witt yelled, so that my eyes did open a second and I grabbed the string of Christmas lights along the eaves, the lights up for years, painted onto the very house, and they slowed me some before I hit the weedy mound of gray clay that leans against the house.

My head is on fire, and I can't see straight. The heat in my forehead is overwhelming. I think I vomit when Rafferty comes back and takes my arm, but I don't remember. I don't remember the rest of the day.

My mother comes and goes. It's the longest afternoon in the history of the world; it holds days and nights in its spell. Everything is dark, indoors. I have the flu.

I fall through the bed for days. My walls are yellow with afternoon, then they roll in brown shadows.

I sleep, wake, sleep, alone. Eddie is sleeping upstairs. My mother brings me a green bottle of 7-Up. I can't hold it in my hand.

A flash. Morning? Is it night? My mother brings a washrag, a thermometer. I dream of being an old man. I go into the schoolyard, but it's the park. My little brother Eddie is coaching a Little League team, but there are no uniforms; the kids mill around the field. I see Parley out there. He's the only one who can catch the ball. I don't recognize anybody else. I go to climb up the bleachers, but I'm too tired, and my body burns. I sit on the first row. I can hear a bunch of kids up on the bleachers behind me. They must be way up there because I can't see them. Parley is leaning against the home-run fence, calling, "I got it! I got it!"

My mother's hands push my hair off my forehead. "How do you feel?"

"Okay."

"You want to try to get up? Something got into you," my mother says. "You've had a bug." Her words are distinct in my empty head; they seem to be printed there. My hearing is different; it's as if I have new ears.

My legs are white in my cutoff Levi's. I feel weak and strange walking over to the park. I'm too tall. I walk on my heels like a chicken. My eyes ache and tear in the broad noon light as I lean my elbows over the home-run fence. But the sun looks familiar, like one I used to know. Something inside my head is trying to come to a balance. I don't know what day it is.

Coach Robbins has the Blue Hats in a practice. He's a good coach, patient; he never yells. He's working with the younger kids on the clay so that next year he'll have an infield. "Take one," I hear him say. "Now take two and cover your bag." In left center, Wedgie Stewart and the other twelve-year-olds are playing Pepper bare-handed. This is our last year.

I stand there and I don't feel like myself. I don't have my mitt, and I don't have my equilibrium. I'm not even here. My shirt is too big. There are wavering lights inside my head, and I can feel the cords in the back of my legs burning tightly. My eyes keep rising shut, and small, smoky flashes tick across the inner surface.

I got something. Something got into me. I had the flu. It's a sickness, a bad cold. It's not time turning me inside out, growing in me like a weed. It's just the flu. It's not time.

8 the all-star

Moisture is offered continually to the human eye through the lacrimal gland in each upper eyelid. Tears are a saline bacterial fluid that are produced in largest quantity when a person cries. It is a physical signal to the body and to others that a person may be hurt.

Today I sleep until noon, but I'm new again, up and ready for planet Earth, and my mother wants to give me grief. She's convinced that I got sick from something down at Witt's. I'm on my bicycle, leaning on one foot. She's sweeping the porch, asking me why I only have one main friend. I tell her I have Rafferty. But, she says, I'm not always going down to Rafferty's morning, noon, and night. She's presenting this topic in such a way that I can understand it is the result of a discussion with my father.

My hands are on the handlebars. My left foot is up on that pedal. I'm looking at my fenderless front tire, the worn square pattern, and I pick a couple of little rocks out of the tread. If I don't say something, she is going to refer openly to my father in a minute.

"Is it all right if I go down to Witt's just today? We're going to play ball."

"Larry, I want you to think it over. There are lots of kids around here your age. It's a good idea to have more than just one friend. Your father is a little worried about how much time you spend down there with Witt. Okay?"

I nod and shrug and rise on one pedal so that the bicycle and I begin to wander down the driveway. I want to appear nonchalant. I scan the park from bandstand to ball field as if I'm looking for a new friend, and I see four clusters of Little Leaguers, practicing. My team works out tomorrow. I can see Rafferty standing with a group of dullards—waiting for Gurber, his corrupt Little League coach, to pop a fly out their way. When Gurber hits one, Rafferty stays in the pack and moves, glove up, toward the catch. His chances, without his glasses, of catching a fly are one in sixty-four thousand. Witt calculated it out, using the diameter of the ball, the size of Raff's mitt, and the area of the field.

But he does look good; he knows how to look like a baseball player. He knows how to stand on one leg with his glove tucked against his waist; how to walk, carrying his glove by the thumb; how to lean on his knees, glove open, looking ready. If he could just see, he'd have it all. Now the season is ending, and though he hasn't been in a single game because Gurber plays his son, Keith, in right field, Rafferty still wants with all of his skinny heart to be an all-star. I know this by the way he puts his first finger in his mouth and his eyes glaze when we talk about it; he wants it worse than anything else in this world. I feel bad, because Rafferty is headed for a fall.

When I round the corner at Concord, I feel my mother's eyes lift from my back, and I bear down and race the wind, all the way to Witt's block. Four gigantic poplars have heaved the sidewalk all around, and there are ramps you can fly from at the right speed.

When I lean my bike in the weeds, I hear a scream. There is a good chance Budd is home throwing the furniture at someone. But his red Buick is not here, so maybe not. I can tell from the high pitch that it's Roto. He stops. I count twelve. He screams again. I count to one hundred and go to the back door. The house is silent except for some scratching I recognize as Atom, probably upstairs on the kitchen table eating the butter.

I hear Witt's voice down in the basement, and Roto screams again, this time a good sharp scream with a little tail on it, which means he's crying. I stand on the broken back step wondering if I might want to locate new friends after all; then I duck down the stairs into the dark. If they are being killed, I guess I want to see it.

I find Witt in the laboratory. Roto is sitting calmly on the table, swinging his legs. Witt is writing something on a page in his clipboard. He shakes his head. "I don't know," he says. He puts down the pencil stub and picks up a greasy pair of pliers.

"Left or right?" Roto says, bored. He sits on the table in the same blue cutoffs he's worn all summer, no shoes or shirt, and his hair, three colors of red, sticks out in one of Budd's special ten-second haircuts. It makes his head look like a cheap soccer ball, lines and all. He is eight years old.

"Left this time."

Roto lifts his left leg straight out. The bottom of his foot is fully tarred. Witt fastens the pliers on each side of his big toe.

"Okay," Roto says. Witt seizes the pliers in both hands and squeezes, jumping a little with the effort. Roto screams, gripping the table as his mouth opens into a square hole as wide as a radio speaker. His teeth are checkered from all the licorice he eats.

After four seconds, Witt drops the pliers on the floor, and they clatter under the table. Roto's mouth closes, but his eyes remain at full bulge for a second or two. When he closes them, two tears squeeze out of each and take dirt all the way to his chin line. As Witt picks up the pencil, a little dust, vibrated by the scream out of the unfinished ceiling, filters down.

"That's five," Roto says happily, jumping onto the floor. He holds his hands out.

"I ought to charge you," Witt says, fishing in his pocket. He hands Roto a dime. "You've got no feelings." But Roto could care less; he's running up the stairs with his cash, headed for the pharmacy and five boxes of Licorice Snaps.

Witt writes for a while, scanning the page up and down with the pencil, and then he stands and throws the whole clipboard across the room into the fruit jars. A mason jar of chili sauce tips and crashes wetly behind the shelves.

"That's no good!" Witt says, finally seeing me. "Five killer crushes and he only cries on two. Two!"

"What'd he do the other three?"

Then Witt really looks at me, realizing I don't know what he's talking about. "You smartass, get up on the table and take off your shoes."

"Thank you, no."

"I should have burned him. I should have had some matches and scorched his arches."

"Your dad counts the matches, remember?"

Witt just glares at me and then wads up his old lab robe and flings it in my face.

Outside I join him on the edge of the geothermal pit, where he sits eating his fingernails. "What were you doing to Roto?"

"It's not Roto. I'm trying to figure out why people cry. I mean, how does pain work?" I can tell by Witt's voice that he has done some thinking about this one. "Why do you cry when you hurt yourself? Why don't people laugh or something else?"

"My dad swears sometimes."

"No, it's this crying. What is crying?" To emphasize the point, Witt kicks his heels hard and a clump of earth cascades upon Atom. "No, it's people. They're too hard to measure. Oh, hell, let it go. It's a mess. Roto's no good; he and Mayreen never cry. Something's wrong with them."

But then he lifts his head and points at me. "But it's something, this crying."

"I thought you'd given up on human behavior."

"I had, but it's everywhere."

I see a new bruise under his ear. "You want to go over to the pharmacy?"

"Yeah, but give it a second so Roto can clear out of there. I'm sick of him today." We stand and he says, "That's what I ought to study." He points down at Atom, buried in the dirt. "Hibernation."

Witt can't let it go. Walking down the alley to the pharmacy, he mutters, "It's something. You ever cry?"

"Yeah."

"When?"

"That time my front wheel came off on the path down by the river and I tore my knee all up."

"Oh, yeah." He's suddenly interested. "How'd it feel?"

I stop, raise my knee, and show him the scar. It looks like a gob of bubble gum the shape of Antarctica. "How'd it feel? It hurt, Witt."

"Yeah, but when else?"

"When else what?"

"When else do you cry?"

Well, I don't want to talk to Witt about crying. I'm not going to tell him when I cry. I'll tell him when I throw my curve in Cup Baseball or some other deep secret, but I am not talking about crying today. But he doesn't know that. He'll talk about anything, even the personal things, because he wants to know. Above all else, he wants to know. I guess that's why he doesn't have any friends besides Rafferty and me.

"I cry when I see Rafferty out in right field trying to play the long ball."

But Witt doesn't hear me now. He's walked on ahead, his head down, his hands in his pockets to the wrists.

Roto is not in the pharmacy. He has already struck here and is probably curled in the willows behind Smalls' sheds, where he gnaws on his Licorice Snaps for an hour at a time. Linda Aikens is in the pharmacy with her mother. They are three rows over, buying shampoo.

It makes me uneasy to see her so close, indoors. The last time Linda and I were indoors together, we danced. I also just received a little square invitation in the actual U.S. mail to Linda's party. She's having a party for our whole class. She told me once in dance class at Edison that she thought we should have one last party, because next fall we would join three other elementary schools in the junior high, and everything would be changed. The party is scheduled for a week from Friday, the last Friday of the summer, the Friday before school starts. Linda also bothers me in an exactly specific way because the last day of school, she asked if she could borrow my algebra book. She only had it a moment, but when I opened it, I found a little blue note: "You're the cutest boy in our class."

I don't want to order root beers until they leave, but Witt orders two frosties right away and Denise sets them before us with a smirk.

"Hello, Lawrence," Mrs. Aikens says to my back.

"Hello, Mrs. Aikens."

"Are you getting ready for school?" Mrs. Aikens doesn't speak to Witt, and Linda is right behind her mother, but she doesn't speak or look at me.

"Not really." What I want to say is, *Please. It's two and a half weeks away. It's still summer.*

"It must be exciting, going to a new school. Linda's looking forward to junior high."

I don't know what to say. "Yeah, I am too." Witt hasn't even turned around to look at them. When they leave, I expect some razing, but he's going forward.

"It isn't just girls, though they do cry." He's holding

his root beer in both hands, off the counter, but he hasn't taken a sip.

I'm worried about Witt. I'm afraid he's going after them, to ask Linda or her mother if she will let him crush her toes with the pliers. In the name of science.

"Oh, great," Rafferty says, coming in, dragging his bat. "Who's buying?"

I'm so relieved to see him that I buy him a root beer. It's the first time I've done such a thing all summer, and it raises Witt from his trance.

"Write that one down in the book, Witt," Rafferty says. "Wait." He turns to me. "Am I going to have to pay for this somehow?"

"Nope."

"Well," he says, hoisting the dripping mug, "I'll remember this, Larry, thanks."

"How's practice?"

"Run and shag. It's okay."

"Rafferty," Witt says, "why do you go to the damn practices?"

I realize it is the hardest question Rafferty's been asked all summer. He has his root beer to his lips, but the glass has stopped tipping and his eyes are roving around a little as he looks for an answer. He hasn't been in one game all season long, but he has not missed a practice. Keith Gurber, the most reluctant baseball player we know, plays right field ahead of Raff. Keith isn't half, not a quarter, of the player Rafferty is. He has a red mitt.

All summer, Witt and I have watched Keith, and he is an ineffective fielder. He stands sideways, near the foul line, deep in right field, offering the fans his narrow profile. Way out there lost in the very corner of the ball field, he looks like a young kid being punished. It's the same at the plate. With the bat heavily on his frail shoulder, he takes his stance: toes together, heels apart, legs straight. Keith averts his eyes, almost facing the umpire. He doesn't want to see what is about to happen.

When the best thing happens and Keith is awarded a walk, Mr. Gurber leans out and bellows from the dugout, "Keith boy! Way to go! Good eye, Keith! Way to watch 'em!"

But for all this, we don't resent Keith. There are a lot of kids who can't or don't play ball; he is just one of them. Unfortunately, he is the one with a coach for a father. Mr. Gurber has played Keith every inning of the fourteen-game schedule and will certainly play him every inning of the last game. Three times during the season, Gurber has taken Rafferty aside and told him not to come to the next evening's game. I guess Rafferty's presence on the bench is some kind of guilt for the guy.

Finally Rafferty puts his root beer mug down on the counter and prints three or four wet rings in front of him. "I go to the practices because they're practices. And I'm on the team." He phrases it carefully because he knows that all Witt is trying to do is get into it again, the old argument about how much he hates Little League. Witt hates it because it's something you have to join, and because parents are involved. He always just mutters, "Organized sports." He says it the way others say "devil worship." But we won't bite anymore. Rafferty has stayed with it the whole season, his last. He's twelve years old. And he's stuck it out because his brother Little Markie, who is eight, is the apple of his mother's eye, and Little Markie is a star on the Brown Hats in the minor leagues. Mrs. Rafferty doesn't miss one of his games. If Little Markie plays before Rafferty's team, then she will stay for part of Raff's game, too. I've seen Rafferty walking alone down the alley in his uniform after a game, holding his mitt like a teddy bear in one hand. And, like I said, from a certain distance, he can look like a baseball player.

"Well," I say, turning on my stool, "one more game, right?"

"I guess," Rafferty says, moving to the lighted dome of the jukebox and his favorite reading of the day.

The bat Rafferty has dragged everywhere this summer, taking it across the handlebars on his bicycle, is a thirty-inch Louisville Slugger with Jackie Robinson's signature pressed into the business end. It is the prettiest bat in the neighborhood, because Rafferty doesn't tap fences or hit rocks or allow Atom the molardog to chew on it. He takes it every time we sleep out. The smooth, blond wood has seen more polishing than any automobile in the neighborhood, but it remains new because, as yet, it is practically unused. Rafferty swings it in batting practice when Coach Gurber is feeling generous or forgetful and lets Rafferty have three pitches, but he rarely taps more than a foul ball. Walking home after practice, he rubs the mark off the end of the bat. He loves that bat.

So later, in Witt's yard, when Witt asks Rafferty again why he insists on continuing in Little League, Rafferty simply swings the bat as an answer. It's a significant swing, initiated high-elbow fashion. The bat floats above his right shoulder and then falls imperceptibly with the little smooth hitch of his left foot as he sidesteps and his weight slides right to left and the wrists race around, winging the bat in a great singing arc as true as a sight line. The Louisville Slugger cuts through the tangible air with a crisp swish, and for the half second the sweet sound lasts, Rafferty looks almost dangerous.

What he is, however, is intent. He stands twisted up by the swing, wound up like so many rags, still looking into blue space above an imaginary center-field fence. His eyes may be lost to this world, but they clearly see another.

"We've got to do something about this boy," Witt says. Rafferty finally drops the pose, unwinds, and stands frankly before us. He's going to say something.

"All-star" is what he says.

"What'd you say?"

"I want to make the all-stars." Rafferty says this as if he's reading from the Bible. I've never heard him say he wanted anything besides food all summer long.

We stare at Rafferty. Witt stares and I stare, and Atom stares up from the geothermal pit.

Rafferty mounts his bike, throws the bat across the handlebars, and starts out, turning back to us to say, "That's all I want."

Witt grabs the seat of Raff's bike, before he can ride off, and pulls him to a stop. "You know you don't get your real dad back if you make the all-stars, right?" Witt has his hand on Raff's shoulder. "He's not coming. He's in Grand Something."

"Grand Junction," Rafferty says. He looks Witt square in the face. "He'll hear about it."

Witt pushes the bicycle so Rafferty wobbles away, headed home, and then he calls, "Everybody would hear about it. Everybody would hear about such a thing."

Witt wants to go over to the schoolyard, and I ride him double all the way between the small gate and up the slope to the tricky bars. He doesn't say much all the way over, just sits still on the crossbar, straining forward. His head smells a little like turpentine.

Mayreen and five or six other kids are winging around on the bars. Mayreen can do six, seven loops, and then a real rangey dead man's fall, landing on her feet. We sit on the bike rack and watch her. I can't understand girls at all, and I guess it starts there at about age nine when they begin doing those circus things on the bars. I couldn't do a dead man's fall if it were an accident, if I were a dead man, falling.

After ten minutes of this observation, my butt gets sore and I ask Witt my favorite question: "What are we doing?"

"It's all right," he answers. "Just wait."

So I wait and watch the weather. Now it rains every afternoon. The clouds roll in, proud and fat, darkening after four and spilling huge and fragrant showers that last an hour. I dread them. They seem the full, round summation of a summer. They say: the weather has changed. They smell like school. In a summer in which I haven't had this feeling once, they make me want to go indoors.

There are five kids flying around. The point of each of their exercises seems to be to leave the Earth. One tiny girl in a torn brown dress climbs eight feet up the jungle gym. Then she leaps across and catches the tallest tricky bar, where she hangs by her arms for a moment, swinging like a flag before dropping on her feet into the sand. Mayreen's friend, a blond girl with two pigtails, is trying to learn Mayreen's tricks, but she balks each time when it comes to letting go of the bar with her knees and flipping in the air. Mayreen is coaching her a little by calling her names, primarily "Chickenshit!"

"Rafferty wants to be an all-star," Witt says.

"Yep. That's what it looks like."

"Are you going to be on the team again?"

"Probably," I say. I was an all-star last year.

"How do they choose them?"

"The coaches pick thirteen and two are elected."

"How do you know?"

"I know."

"Elected?"

"Yeah, by the players on all the teams."

"When?"

"After the last game, day after tomorrow. In the dugouts. But you can forget that; no one even knows Rafferty's name."

Witt turns to me and says, "Yet. They don't know his name yet." And then he turns back to the gymnastics and says, "Elected. Okay." He's nodding. "Okay, okay, okay."

I leave the bike rack and go sit against the old school building. This is the Edison Elementary School that I attended for seven years, counting kindergarten. The school is named after Thomas Alva Edison, and I remember the day that the librarian, Mrs. Henderson, opened the library safe and showed us the original letter from Mr. Edison saying how pleased he was that they had chosen to name the school after him. I thought it was a great letter and resolved to do something someday to get a school named after me. It won't be this summer.

Finally the girl who has been trying to learn the dead man's fall from Mayreen tries it. We watch her loop out, letting the bar go. She swings too far, straightens her legs too soon, and lands flat on her back. She hits with a sound like a door being slammed in another part of the house.

"Come on," Witt says, and he's away to the rescue.

But when I join him, he's not rescuing anything. He stands directly over the girl, his hands on his knees, studying her face, which has gone gray. She is not making one sound. I listen and there isn't even a whimper.

"Now watch," Witt says to me. "Watch this."

Her eyes swell and wander in her gray face. Her mouth is working a little, open, close, open, close, like a fish. Her lips are slightly blue. I realize that we are watching her die. Witt hasn't moved.

Then there is a raw little moaning, so low that at first I turn, thinking it is coming from the other side of the school, but with a wet pop, it roars open, into a wicked wheeze drawn backward in the girl's throat. It lasts half a minute, and toward the end, her eyes close, and the sound becomes just wind. Her chest has ballooned crazily like some ten-cent doll, and, after a moment of silence, she exhales. It starts with a flat explosion of saliva that drives even Witt back from his observation point. On her second breath, the girl moves. She rolls to her side and curls up, and Witt steps over her so he can still have a full view of the face. I'm standing behind him. It is now that she starts crying. Her eyes shudder erratically in fits of recovery, and her body shakes as she cries. She's rubbing her eyes and crying, tossing in a little scream once in a while, but no real words we can make out. She cries and cries. After a few seconds, I've observed all I care to, and I go back over to the bike rack, but Witt is still standing there. His ankles are the only thing the girl can see. It's going to be a twenty-minute session, but after five or so, Witt turns and walks slowly back to me. Mayreen, who has done three more bold dead man's falls during this interlude, has taken his place. I hear her say, "Oh, shut up, Shawnee, you chickenshit!"

The clouds have really come in now, full and dark, and the air smells of earth and trees. The light has shifted into a clear dusk, and everything appears more distinct. When it rains, we usually go into Witt's basement and play a game in the bottle-cap league, but today I don't feel like it. I watch the kids risking their lives. They're really cranking through their tricks now, frenzied by the coming rain.

Witt is on high alert for the next falling girl. I pull my bike out of the rack and drift down the schoolyard, waving once at Witt. My mother will be glad to see me home early. The rain hits as I'm taking the corner on Nevada Avenue, and I see all the kids in the summer crafts program scurry onto the park bandstand. By the time I lean my bicycle on our patio, I'm soaked.

From where I sit in the living room, I can see the whole park taking the rain. The trees have all turned black and they ride a little in the weather. It's dark enough inside to turn on a light, but I sit in the brown darkness, looking out.

I loved my old school. I loved Miss Miller and Miss Talbot and Miss Vincent and even Mrs. Tu, the principal. She taught our class how to draw apples when I was in the fourth grade. I even loved the old lavatory without doors on the stalls. You could stand against the end of the mirror and raise your foot and wave your hand and make it look like you were flying. Those days are gone. Outside I can see Little Markie and one of his pals walking through the puddles in the infield.

"What are you doing home?" My mother has come upstairs from the laundry room.

"Nothing."

I don't see Rafferty for two entire days. It's like he's hiding out, and then he appears wearing his all-star cap.

He comes down the stairs into Witt's basement, where Witt and I are right in the middle of drilling the bat. Witt cranks the killer auger slowly while I try to hold the nervous, binding bat in my hands. Every four rotations, Witt removes the one-inch bit and checks to see that he's still in line. To Rafferty, it must look as though we're trying to open a long, wooden bottle of wine.

"What are you guys doing?" he says.

He doesn't know that we're reaming out his most precious possession. He thinks that we just borrowed his bat, not that we're changing it forever. He doesn't know that we went to his house, his room, the very night he was elected to the all-stars and stole his glasses as well, and that we have just spent two hours dismantling the frames and taping the lenses into two short cardboard tubes, a treacherous pair of goggles. Rafferty doesn't know anything. To keep it that way, Witt quietly takes the bat from my hands and sets it behind two tires.

Suddenly, in the poor light, I sense something different about Rafferty. I can't see his face; it's his posture. He's slumped against the wall; his head is down. The white button on the top of the cap is pointed right at me.

"Hey." I go over to him.

His head doesn't move, but his eyes, under his brows,

come up to me. His lower lip swells.

"Hey, what's the matter, all-star?"

His lip quivers. "What are you guys doing?" he says again. But his voice is way too tight, and I see his jawbone clench, ease, and clench again. Rafferty's going to cry.

"What's the matter, Raff?"

He's looking at me, holding his eyes steady, but they're going to boil over, I can tell. This is not too good. Maybe he has seen what we were doing to his bat.

Witt comes over. He's dragging the auger drill like an old snake. Witt swings the bit end up and presses his thumb on the sharp cone point.

Rafferty starts, "I'm . . . a . . ."

"He's scared," Witt says, handing me the huge drill.

"He's got the hat." Witt pulls it off Rafferty's head and rotates it on his finger. I've got one just like it at home; they passed them out last night. It has a red bill and a blue peak and is shot through with white lines and three sizes of stars. It looks like the little flag of some crazy country, a country ready for revolution. It looks a lot like something you could buy at the fair. "And what a hat." He snugs it back on Rafferty, good and crooked. "Yeah, he's got the hat now, but he's scared."

"Scared?" I say. "You're scared?" Rafferty's head is

starting to nod up and down, up and down, in a rapid movement that he is using to fight the tears.

"Well, there's nothing to be scared about now, all-star," Witt says. "We're fixing everything." Witt takes the drill back from me. "When is practice?"

"Right away."

"Great. Well, look, will you try something?"

"Sure." Rafferty sounds relieved.

"Wear these." Witt snags the goggles out of his back pocket. They look like a real gross lucky charm. "They're baseball glasses. You'll need them on the all-stars. In right field, and at the plate. Okay?"

"Okay."

We all climb outside, and Rafferty snaps the goggles onto his face. The strap is seven linked rubber bands. He looks like a lost frogman. In the daylight, the all-star cap really comes to life. "What's that?" he says. He's pointing at the television aerial on Smalls' sheds, which has been there five years. His head swivels in wonder at all the new sights. "Geez," he says. "These really work."

Witt takes him by the shoulders. "And Rafferty. We're fixing your bat, okay? It will be ready for the game tomorrow."

"Sure, sure," Rafferty says. He can see so much that

he's barely listening. He's on his bike now, cruising down Concord, headed for practice an hour early, his head scanning rooftops, trees, backyards, the entire universe.

"Good luck," Witt yells. "Good luck, you all-star."

Downstairs in the laboratory, Witt realigns the drill atop the bat and turns it slowly. The wooden heart of the Louisville Slugger peels out around the auger in thin, blond curls.

"Rafferty's an all-star," I say. Some skinny kid who couldn't see across the infield, a kid who hasn't played a third of an inning all season long as a twelve-year-old, has been elected to the all-star team by the votes of his fellow players.

"Yep," Witt says, concentrating on the core of the bat. "He deserves it." In another tone he adds, "He wanted it."

The night before the last league game, Witt stenciled VOTE RAFFERTY—ALL-STARS throughout the two green dugouts in white spray paint. It was particularly effective because the only writing the Little Leaguers had been used to seeing in the dugouts was a hideous, carved "Fuck You" in the home dugout and a green Magic

Marker slogan, "Up your gigi with a ten-foot pole!" in the visitors'. Confronted with Rafferty's name in bold white letters, even printed on the benches, and confused by the rumor that Rafferty was in reality a large kid on the Gold Hats who already, at age twelve, had a beard, the players voted heavily for him.

"And he has to play in the game."

"Right. At least for a minute. That's the rule for all-star games."

Our game is Friday afternoon at one o'clock. Edison League, which is our league, is playing against a team from clear across town, the all-stars from Holladay. I'm starting at second base.

After five more turns, Witt pinches the bit at the top of the bat and removes it. Looking at the measure on the drill, we see we're in just over seven inches, right down the center. Witt starts up again. It takes half an hour until he's buried the bit, and the shank is rankling the top of the bat. We've gone as far as we can. The table is covered with a mound of golden spirals of wood. I tip the bat and tap out the sawdust. Emptied, the bat weighs a few ounces. After I wave it around like a wand, Witt takes it from me and puts his eye to the hole in the top as if it is a telescope.

"I think we're all right," he says. "The Piston Bat, the only Piston Bat on this or any planet whatsoever." He says it in capital letters.

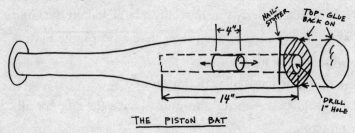

THE PISTON BAT

We pour two tablespoons of baby powder in the cavity.

"Graphite is a better lubricant," Witt says. Then he goes back into the secret recesses of his room and returns with a four-inch length of steel pipe. He hands it to me. "Lead would be better," he says. "But file the ends of this." While I'm filing the pipe, Witt bores a small hole across the fat top of the bat.

"Hurt or scared," he says. "That's all there is."

"What is?" I hand him the smooth pipe.

"Why people cry. I got it. You see Raff?" He lowers the metal pipe into the bat; it fits exactly, and when he drops it, it disappears. Next he clips the head off a ten-penny nail using his wire cutters, and he inserts the nail in the little hole as a crossbar at the very top to keep the pipe from blasting out the end. He tips the bat upside down, the pipe slips—*tink!*—against the nail, a puff of powder emerges, and Witt smiles.

"People get hurt or scared and they cry. I've got that. Why they don't do something else, I don't know, and," he adds, grabbing the putty, "I don't care." He takes his pocketknife and covers the nail hole with putty. "I used to cry sometimes," Witt says. "But now I don't need to anymore. I'm done." We glue the wooden cap back on the end of the bat with too much Elmer's Glue-All, wipe it off, and Witt holds it up in the light. It looks just like a bat again.

After the final all-star practice late in the day, Raff and I hang out, sitting against the Maltair Bowling Lanes sign on the home-run fence. He's taken the goggles off and they've left perfect, sharp, red circles around his eyes.

"Nice catch."

"Yeah," he says, working his mitt. He's not going to form a pocket in it this late. He's had it four years and it still opens and shuts like a book. I don't think it's made of leather. He looks at me with new confidence. "Did you see me catch that fly ball? These goggles do the trick."

Behind the fence on the green, Grant and Max

Starkey, the twins, have started up their big, red, gas airplane, and it is buzzing in large circles. The twins come to the park every week with another of their new toys; they're the richest kids in our neighborhood. The plane's roar gathers a crowd of kids who stand and watch.

I can see Witt over there leaning on Rafferty's bat, watching the mob. He knows that if enough kids gather with nothing much to do, somebody will end up crying, and he can do a little research. Lately he's been following Benny and Cling around while they bully the kids out of nickels for cigarettes. Down by the swings they stand in the way until they get a pocketful of spare change, or they hold the teeter-totter until some kid pays the toll or starts crying.

Finally I see what is going to happen. Benny and Cling are working the little crowd pretty hard, throwing kids aside like coats. Over and under everything is the awesome buzzing of the plane, and somebody is going to get pantsed. Benny and Cling finally settle on Keith Gurber. They drag him away a few yards by his feet as if they are going to eat him, and they throw his shoes at the plane, laughing. Keith is pleading pretty hard, but they dump him out of his pants, and Benny runs over and tosses them up on the Little League scoreboard. That's when I see Eddie up there, where he's been watching our practice. I hate for my brother to see this stuff. Now Keith is crying. Nobody's going near him until Benny and Cling decide to leave. He just lies there curled on the grass in his shorts, crying into his fists. Witt is there, of course, observing.

When Benny and Cling walk by us, we don't move. It is better to stand your ground than to show any fear. Besides, they remember us from the rock fight. Cling slinks by in his best humanoid manner. My heart rages as he passes; I am deeply and forever scared of him. Benny pauses and smiles. "Nice hats, boys." He laughs down in his throat and moves on, toward the swings and more mayhem.

In all the vast possibilities of summertime, those two guys are the only terror I know. Every time I see them, my stomach flickers. Sooner or later, Cling is going to bother Eddie, and I'm going to have to fight him, and I know he's going to beat me up. My father told me one night over the dinner table that the one time a person had to fight was to defend his brothers. I'd been picking on Eddie, and he told me to save it for any hoodlum who bothered my brother. Now every time I see Eddie headed for the park, I start worrying. I know he doesn't have a nickel to give them if they start shoving, and I know that I don't really know how to fight.

I see Eddie pull the pants free from the scoreboard and throw them down to Keith. He seems unaware of the terrible dangers in the universe, and the only thing I can hear him say is "Hey, Keith, put your pants back on."

"Hey, all-stars." Witt has come up along the back of the fence. When he reaches us, he lifts Rafferty's bat over and hands it to him. "All fixed," he says.

"What'd you find out?" I motion over to where Keith is pulling on his pants.

"Not much. Keith got scared."

Rafferty backs away from the fence and takes his stance. As he swings, the bat leaps out on its own and snaps around in a deadly slash that amazes even him. He has trouble holding on to it. As it cuts the air, the bat makes a little noise, that *tink!*

"What'd you do?"

Witt takes the bat back and says, "We made one mistake on the prototype." He quickly inverts the bat and we hear again: *tink!* as the pipe hits the nail. He speaks to me: "Next time we'll buffer that with a dowel."

"Prototype?" Rafferty says, grabbing the bat back and

shaking it. *Tink! Tink! Tink!* "Prototype!"

"Just use it, Raff," Witt says. "It's a bat for an all-star."

The only Little League games that are played at one in the afternoon are the opening game the last week in May and the all-star games, which are played in late August, and these are extravaganzas. The park is a circus. You can hardly see the swings. The pennants along the backstop make it look like somebody's selling used cars. Just after noon the music starts waving out of the press box as everybody's mother arrives to wipe the counters and start up the snow-cone machine.

The Holladay mothers arrive early and put up a paper banner that says SUPPORT HOLLADAY LITTLE LEAGUERS. The Holladay team arrives in a van. The players step out casually, and they look good. Instead of four colors, like ours, their uniforms are only gray and white. They look real sober, like pros, like this is just one stop on an unending baseball tour in which they have humiliated teams from here to Midvale. I feel funny watching them climb out of the van and begin to warm up. They are not that much bigger than we are, but they arrange themselves in measured rows and begin to toss brand-new baseballs back and forth. It looks like a drill. I notice they all wear polished black shoes with rubber cleats.

Our all-stars arrive one at a time on their bikes. In our tricky hats and various-colored tennis shoes, we look a lot like small-time vendors at this carnival. But slowly enough of us gather to seem like a team, and Wedgie Stewart, our best player, has even brought a baseball. It's covered with black electrician's tape, but we fan out in a rangy mob and start throwing it around, calling one another's names frantically in order to receive it maybe once every fifteen minutes. Screaming like that and grouped in what appears to be a nine-pointed star, hurling a black sphere each to each, our all-stars appear kind of dangerous. The Holladay kids stop warming up to witness the ritual.

Coach Gurber sits on the front row of the bleachers in his coaching shirt. Keith sits beside him in civilian clothes, waiting for the chance to escape and climb trees down by the bandstand. Poor Keith hates baseball; it hasn't been very good to him. Luckily for Rafferty, Gurber is not the all-star coach. His team came in last. The all-star coach is Robbins, whose Blue Hats won the league. Robbins is a young guy, a good ball player himself, but what really qualifies him to coach, in my opinion, is that he doesn't have kids. When he arrives, we all-stars swarm around him, and he spills out the baseballs before us as if he is feeding fish.

I can see Witt at his old place, behind the backstop, fingers in the chain link, guarding the Piston Bat, which leans against the fence beside him. When I catch his eye, he shakes his head sadly and I can almost hear him: "Organized sports." He wants me to think he's down here to see if his invention is going to work. He wants everybody to think he's here in the name of science, but I can see a smile under his expression. He's down here to give Raff a little boost, and he's excited like the rest of us. He's down here because we're all friends.

Coach Robbins calls us all into the dugout, where we give one group cheer and take the field. I haven't noticed anything wrong, but when I take my position at second and start fielding practice grounders from Lopez, the first baseman, I see Witt slap his hands against the side of his face in anguish. I signal him: what? He points to right field. I turn and see Rafferty trot into place. Oh, no.

Witt is thinking the same thing I am: Rafferty has made a mistake; he's going to embarrass himself. I look at Mrs. Rafferty in her place on the second row. She sits there, arms folded, beside Rudy the Unworthy. Oh, no. Rafferty did this once, early in the season, and before the first pitch of the game, the umpire had to stop everything and ask Coach Gurber why there were two players in right field. That time Gurber lost his head. He jumped the fence and started windmilling his arms for Rafferty to get the hell back here—what did he think he was doing! Watching Rafferty shuffle back across the infield that day, his head between his shoulders, was just as much as I could take. Now, again, I check Mrs. Rafferty. She is exquisite. She doesn't have her hands over her face, like last time. In fact, she is standing up, along with the whole crowd, her hand over her heart. I look back to right field. There is only one kid out there, his flashy cap over his heart for "The Star-Spangled Banner." It is the goggled Rafferty.

Robbins is required to play everybody, so I guess he's risking Rafferty first, or else he just doesn't know who Rafferty is. Anyway, I have to smile. Rafferty waves at me. He looks like a raccoon.

Dickey is throwing for us. He's a good pitcher for a kid with one pitch, a low fastball. He is able to ground three men out in seven pitches. Two of the grounders are hit to me at second, which means the Holladay kids are behind Dickey a little. It'll take a couple innings, at least, for them to get on him.

The Holladay pitcher is a skinny kid who throws

sidearm. He, too, basically has one pitch, also a fastball, but it leaves his hand low and rises a bit crossing the plate. I love to swing, and he strikes me out on three close high pitches. It is like trying to hit a bird with a hammer. I hear Witt groan with each swish.

Nearly three innings go by just like that, strikeouts and grounders, when, as the second batter in the third inning, Rafferty is the first person in the ball game to reach first base. He has the bat on his shoulder, but he never has a chance to use it. It seems that they all know who Rafferty is. Witt yells, "Come on, Rafferty!" and the pitcher takes one more deep look at those goggles and steps back from the mound. The entire infield clusters around him. I don't think anything about it until the players have returned to their positions, and the pitcher steps hard and throws his sidearm fastball right into Rafferty's head. We hear it hit, and it sounds just like a hardball hitting bone. Rafferty stays right in his stance as the ball rebounds all the way to third base. Then I remember Rafferty's name painted all over the dugout. They've read about him and are afraid he's our ace. Rafferty looks back at the ump and steps across the plate to take his walk, before collapsing like an empty flour sack softly onto the baseline.

We all run out and gather around Rafferty. The stitches of the baseball are distinctly printed in red across his temple. His mother runs out and holds his head in her beautiful hands. When he opens his eyes, he sits right up and says to Robbins, "Coach, please, don't take me out. I can hit this guy." One whole side of his face is white from the chalk of the baseline. Two players help Rafferty to first, where he stands, hands on knees, wavering, but not seriously.

Rafferty is stranded on first, and in the top of the fourth I go out on the field and give Rafferty his mitt and wait to see if Robbins is going to take him out. No way. Like everyone else who was there when Rafferty came to, evidently the coach hasn't heard anything that crazy all summer. Rafferty is in to stay.

Before the inning commences, Dickey comes out to second and asks me if he should take down a couple of their guys.

"Don't do it," I tell him. "No matter how hard you hit them, they still get first base." Dickey holds his own. He's keeping his fastball low, and we haven't had anything but limping grounders and one loopy line drive to deep short. He's only walked one guy.

So it all keeps until the sixth and final inning. After

our leadoff man strikes out, Rafferty comes to the plate. He's magnificent. With his stances and his adjusting those goggles and his sweet practice swings, each with a metallic click that only Witt and I can hear, Rafferty looks like a hired assassin. I can see Witt clipped against the backstop, his fingers through the fence. Mrs. Rafferty sits in the second bleacher row, Rudy the Intruder spellbound beside her, but now her arms have unfolded and her hands are clutching the bench.

"Go ahead, Rafferty!" I yell from the dugout. It is a full pleasure to call his name. "Hit this guy!"

The first pitch is a sidearm brushback that would have sent most kids running for the dugout in tears. It would have affected me. Rafferty lifts his chin to let the ball pass. During the windup for the next pitch, Rafferty steps out of the box. The Holladay pitcher aborts the pitch awkwardly, stepping on his own left foot, and then tries to save face by casually throwing the ball to the first baseman, who isn't looking. The ball goes into right field. There is laughter. Some of it is from me, I admit. Rafferty is in control. I can see Witt talking to him. Finally Rafferty taps his tennis shoes with the Piston Bat and steps into the box, snapping into his stance before the Holladay pitcher even has the ball back.

The next pitch is thrown by a less confident person than we've seen all day. Rafferty's head leans toward it, and he strides, hitching the bat faintly as his swing begins. The bat starts slowly, gracefully, but then I hear the *tink!* as the piston shoots out, and the rest of the swing is savage. Rafferty connects with the ball in front of the plate, and he pulls it right down the line into left field. It's a line shot, and I mean shot, three feet over the third baseman's head. The crowd, which has been sweating murder for two hours, explodes. I've never heard anything like it in this park in which I have spent my lifetime. The ball streams straight as a nail, no rise or fall, as Rafferty rounds first, headed for second. It could be a home run, I think at first; then the ball slams into the wooden fence six inches from the top of the Nickel's Market sign. Any other ball in that spot would have been a double, but this hit is so sharp that the baseball rebounds all the way back in and is finally fielded by the shortstop as Rafferty pulls up at third, standing.

He stands on the base, just like a pro, his hands on his hips, his head cocked up as if he is waiting for something to happen. He's been practicing all summer, all the summers I have known him, to stand on third base this way. The four hundred people in the park, even the little kids down by the swings and those who were playing tennis, seem to be jumping up and down, screaming. The Holladay team is squirming, their coach is pacing, their batboy runs in little circles. I hear something strange, gutteral and sharp, and I turn to see Rudy jumping up and down and clapping and simply bellowing like a demon there beside Mrs. Rafferty.

Meanwhile Rafferty himself is the only person standing still in all this roaring noise. Witt is three feet off the ground on the backstop fence. Mrs. Rafferty is standing, clapping. When I see Coach Gurber jumping on the bleachers, waving his hat and hollering, I have to sit down. The tumult lasts four or five minutes. It stops the game.

In fact, the tumult never really stops. Even when the next two hitters strike out and we go into extra innings, there is a general subsurface roar that I've never heard before. Rafferty has stopped the park. Even kids who were in trees on the other side of the bandstand have pressed into the out-of-play fence and are watching the game.

In the seventh, we have trouble. Dickey walks one guy. I give him third base on a fielder's choice, and he scores on a fly out to center. I'm up in the bottom of the inning, and I'm scared. All I want is to get on base. I'm willing to put my head in front of the ball just so I don't strike out, which I've done twice already. As I stand in the on-deck circle, I see that the afternoon has fallen apart, the clouds have come up as if to see me go down swinging, and I find myself wishing for rain. The air thickens. After Lopez grounds out to the pitcher, I step up. Grace is with me, for the second pitch is inside and I shear it off the handle between first and second base for a single.

When you stand on first base in the last Little League game of your life in what seems to be the last day of summer ever, and all the people you know are gathered in a group behind the fences as if to have their assembled picture taken, it all can make you feel quite old. As I stand here now, I feel as if first base is outer space and I am looking down from two hundred miles. From my vantage point, I look down and see the next two kids strike out, and then see the crowd heave together one last time as our team gathers to cheer the victors, and Rafferty's mother gathers him in the hug he's been waiting for all summer. Then the motorcylist Rudy the Muscular hoists him onto his shoulders and they turn in the gray air three or four times. Rafferty goes home with them, as the citizens of my world drift from the park in groups. My parents come over, and my mother straightens my cap, and my dad takes my picture. I tell them I'll be home in a while. Eddie says, "What'd you guys do to Rafferty's bat?" When they turn and walk home, I jog back across the diamond.

The first rain hits across the dry infield, ripping dust like a machine gun. The rain makes my uniform smell like wool, a smell, if you think about it, that is a lot like the end of the season. I walk into the empty visitors' dugout. Witt is sitting down at the end in the dark. Around him like wallpaper print, the VOTE RAFFERTY— ALL-STARS stencils stand out in the gloom. Witt has the bat in his hand, and he's turning it like a baton to hear the click of the piston.

"Nice hit," he says.

"It was off the handle."

"I know, but it went through the hole: base hit."

I sit down, smelling like wool. "Some Rafferty," I say.

"Some bat," Witt says, clicking the piston a few times. "You see Rafferty on third?"

"Yeah."

"You know what he looked like?" Witt is smiling, leaning back against the printed wall. "He looked like a statue of Zorro. Those goggles. Didn't he? The masked hero." He quickly makes a big Z in the air with the bat.

The rain has settled in now, drumming the dugout roof, pooling in a low spot by second.

"Well, that's Little League," I say.

Witt grins at me. "This version," he says. "That's this version."

9 at the hop

Music is sound arranged in patterns. Many of these patterns have mathematical and geometric roots. Music is used in ceremony, work, and entertainment to offer listeners a sense of mystery, relief, and distance from the ordinary world.

Drying off from the shower, I'm trying to sing the most popular song of the year, which is heaping with words that all rhyme with *going* or *boring*, I can't tell. I whip the towel around my arms and legs. I cannot sing, but I have heard this insistent ditty on the radio, and it has me hooked. I never even listened to the radio last spring, and now I find myself listening all the time. My dad framed the radio in the wall when he built our basement. I turn the volume up and fall back on our bed and do a backward somersault naked to dry my back.

Hopping up to grab some underwear, I find something different on my bureau. I've been finding these clippings out of *Ladies' Home Journal* for a while now. My mother cuts them out and puts them on my bureau. They're about things like "Surviving the Troublesome Teens" and "The Six Teenage Dangers." I try not to touch them. I don't move them or go near my bureau top while they're up there. After four or five days they disappear. My mother and I have never talked about them.

The last one, a few weeks ago, was titled "What Teenagers Want to Know About SEX." The word *sex* was stenciled in red block letters on a picture of a big wooden crate, the kind they must keep dynamite in. I don't want any of it. What are they trying to do, embarrass everybody in the whole world? For that week I gave my bureau plenty of room. I didn't change my underwear for three days, and when the article disappeared, I finally felt free to sleep late the next day.

Standing there with one leg in my shorts, I see the pamphlet on my bureau. Picking it up, I read, *Understanding Puberty*. Oh my God.

I drop it like a firecracker. What a word: *puberty*. It should be in the Pledge of Allegiance: "with puberty and justice for all." The truth is, I don't even know exactly what it is. They showed that film last June to all the girls while the boys were kept in Mr. Compton's class.

And now my mother is leaving pamphlets on my bureau. I can already see it: next she'll start leaving whole books and stacks of books. I don't need this; it is not working.

I snap on my undershorts and go back to the pamphlet. *Understanding Puberty*. It could be a travel brochure. Inside I see the diagram of the male reproductive organs. It all looks a lot like Florida, the capital of which is Tallahassee. Two pages later are the female reproductive organs, the side view, internal. It looks like nothing, like lines, like instructions for something terrible. I try to picture Linda Aikens or Karen Wilkes looking anything like this, and the truth is, my imagination won't work. No wonder sex is such a big secret: it's brutal. And this is just the puberty part. A couple of pages later I read, "Adolescents are torn by the violent distractions of puberty. . . ." My mother calls down the stairs, "Larry, don't be late!" I drop the pamphlet again as my heart explodes and my face heats up.

"I won't! I'm coming!" I call back, but my voice is changed, all throaty, so now she knows for sure.

I spend the next five or ten minutes trying to remember

exactly how the little book was originally sitting on the bureau. I adjust it an eighth of an inch at a time, trying to get it just right. Then I pick it up again and wipe my fingerprints off the glossy cover, but the towel is wet and leaves a little smear, so I toss it back up on the dresser and try again to turn it around so it looks untouched.

Then I take it down and check out the female reproductive organs again. I can see the buttocks, but the rest is a horrifying puzzle. This time, when I replace it, I see that the cover is bent, so I leave it there all wrong and sit on my bed, sick right through the heart. By this time I don't even want to go to the party.

The song on the radio now is "Something, something, drive something away!" I sit on my bed and pull on the first pair of long pants I've worn all summer, not counting my baseball uniform. My mother bought them for me as part of my school clothes. The pants are chocolate-brown corduroy, and when I stand up and brush my hand on the leg, they feel wonderful. I run my new brown belt with the small brass buckle through the loops. Tucking in my white shirt, rolling up the sleeves, and buckling the belt, I feel better. I actually feel mature. Maybe that was puberty I just passed through. My hair is too short to comb, but I comb it anyway, just to see if I look right doing it.

"Drive yourself away!" the song cries. "Something, something, ba-bay." I'm not the kind of person who will ever be able to call any girl my age *ba-bay*. I would never even say the word that way, but when I listen to this music, I sing right along, convinced. How does music work on you that way? I want to ask Witt, but then I'd be exposed as a guy who sings, "Ba-bay, ba-bay, drive something, something." The pamphlet glows in the dark. I fold it in half and stuff it in the back pocket of my new trousers. I button the pocket.

Upstairs in the kitchen, my mother looks at me and says, "Well, hello, Mister. Who might you be?"

"Yeah," I say. "Rafferty and I are going to walk over to the class party."

"Stan, come in here," my mother calls.

My father comes in the kitchen. He is carrying my little brother Ricky. "Say, you look pretty good, Larry. What is this, a party?"

"Yeah, Rafferty and I are going to walk over to the class party."

"Isn't Witt going?"

"Naw. He doesn't go to many things like this."

"Witt is dropping out of school," Eddie says. He sneaks up behind me and rubs the leg of my corduroys.

"He is?" asks my mother.

"No, he's not!" I say to her. "Eddie doesn't know anything." I don't know about this. I rode by Witt's house twice last week, but the red Buick was there and I didn't stop. Something's going on.

"Roto said so," Eddie goes on. "He said there was a big fight and Witt ran away. He's in Idaho. He's not going to school."

I say, "There you go. You're getting your information from Roto." My mother brushes my hair back, but finally I see Rafferty's silhouette outside our screen door and I escape.

We walk across the park, and Rafferty is all hot to tell me about his new life. Since baseball ended, he's been going over to Jordan Community Swimming Pool and hanging out with Ivan Kidder and Tim Torkelson. "You know what we saw?" I don't have to answer; he's going on. "We saw Josie Herron's hairs. She wears this weird red bathing suit, and if you walk by her chair, you can see her hairs. Talk about a turn-on. You gotta get over there before the week's over."

"Okay, I'll try," I say, and I hear it as the most significant lie I've told all summer. When we're halfway across the park, I ask him, "Is Witt dropping out of school?"

"I don't know anything about Witt. He's pissed me from day one," Rafferty says. "Roto said that his old man pounded him good or something, an extra portion. I heard he broke his arm. I think Budd found that old razor clogged from when Witt shaved the stupid cat. Why didn't he hide the stupid razor? Can't Witt hide anything? For a genius, he's an idiot."

Rafferty is wearing glasses again. They're not his old glasses but new ones he got for school. The frames are little chrome girders, and they make Rafferty look ready for the new age. "They're cool, right? Rudy took me down to Sears and helped me pick them out."

I look him over. *Rudy helped him pick these glasses.* Early last week while Witt and I played Targets off the railroad trestle, we saw Rafferty cruise by on the back of Rudy the Barbarian's motorcyle. Witt had said to me quietly, "Rafferty's a goner." And he may be. I know for a fact that he's ridden on the motorcycle he flipped off. Now, as we walk toward the class party, he seems a lot different from the blind kid I swindled all summer. He's wearing a red shirt, short sleeves, and chinos. I haven't seen him in a button shirt in my whole life.

Linda Aikens lives just across the river from the

junior high. It's a good walk because most of the way you can stay by the river and throw rocks at the passing debris. It's just getting dark when we walk down the flagstone steps into the junior-high schoolyard. The asphalt here is crisscrossed by a complicated series of lines painted in yellow paint. There are several gigantic intersecting circles. The entire yard is, in fact, a diagram of our futures, and it makes my stomach feel the same way the diagram of the female reproductive organs did. I take the pamphlet out and hand it to Rafferty.

"Check this out."

He takes it and turns a few pages, still walking. It's funny to see him read without holding the paper against his nose. He hands it back. "Wonderfully informative."

"My mother left it for me."

"Your mother? That is sad."

"Right." We walk by the gymnasium. Someone has thrown a bottle of ink against the brick siding, and a blue stain flashes dead center. The whole school seems to be watching me. In five days I'll come here as a student.

"You ever see Benny's magazines?" Rafferty asks.

"Not really."

"You haven't, have you? Do you know about them? I mean, they show everything." It's becoming a long day for me. All this noise. I try to keep walking.

"You went over to Benny's." Since their clubhouse crashed into the alley, they made a kind of lean-to against a fence where they go to look at their magazine stash now.

"Yeah, I went over. They've got a stack of the stuff. You can learn a lot about the way women work over there. He's got some genuine magazines." Raff shrugs like an expert. "And Rudy's been telling me some stuff."

"I'll bet," I say. Actually I gave Benny some magazines over a year ago. I found them in the vacant lot. Somebody had thrown them out of a car and they had blown into Roto's fort. I remember one picture. It showed a woman sitting at a glass table as if she was about to eat a bowl of peaches. She had huge, featureless breasts that fell over onto the table in two great heaps. At that time it had seemed the most hilarious photograph I had ever seen. And, even in retrospect, it seemed that someone had been out to make fun of the woman. I could hear the photographer pleading, "Come on, now lean forward and flop your tits up on the table and give them a rest."

"I'll tell you, it beats hanging out with Witt all day long, playing stupid games, experiments, dreaming. This makes all his science one big stupid joke. This is something real, man. It makes you feel all lit up."

"Right."

"And then you can go back whenever you want and see the magazines."

"If you join." I want to ask him if there is a password.

"Yeah, you have to join, but it's great. Hey, we're going to this school this year. It is a new world. You can't play games all your life. He sure screwed my bat." Rafferty's walked on ahead.

We go down the grassy slope to the walk bridge across the river, and I look at Rafferty in his new glasses and that red shirt, and I hardly know him. This kid used to be a friend of mine, I think. And now I spot another difference: this Rafferty is two inches taller than I am. That wasn't true at the beginning of the summer. His face is different, too, in a way I can't describe except to say it seems to have more separate parts. His eyebrows have grown together over his nose.

On the walk bridge we stop and I lean over the rail and fold *Understanding Puberty* in half again and again and then twist it into a fat cigar and release it over the river. It hits the water right alongside a white quart bottle that glints once coming out from under the bridge, and we hurry and ramble after it along the ruined river trail, throwing rocks as fast as we can find them. Rafferty finally swamps the bottle by heaving a boulder the size of a skull right next to it. It's not as satisfying as hearing glass break and watching a bottle really go down, but we stand there in the thicket, breathing, and for a moment, it's just like old times; we're just dressed differently.

"Hey," Rafferty says, pointing, "check that!" There across the river, high in a tree that is dead from the waist up like so many of the giant trees along the river, hangs the old bra. Rafferty laughs. The bra is outlined perfectly against the last yellow tinge in the purple sky; it has been there forever. "Think of that," he says. "Think of what went in that."

"I can imagine," I lie. I can't imagine. I can't imagine how it ever got up there. I've never seen anything so wrong, so out of place.

On the way back to the bridge, Rafferty asks, "Are you going to dance?"

"I don't know. Are you?"

"You kidding? Name one girl in our class who isn't a skag."

Linda's house is a long, low, brick deal, much nicer than anything in our neighborhood. I've seen pictures of places like this in magazines, and they are called "ranch houses," for some reason. The brick walkway up to her front door is curved, and they have a miniature street lamp in the front yard. It's a stupid idea, because it ruins what could have been a decent Sock Ball field. The front door has an *A* in it, and Mrs. Aikens welcomes us in.

There are a bunch of kids in the kitchen, which spills out through a large sliding-glass door onto a patio. The kids in the kitchen are mainly girls, and the kids on the patio are mainly boys. Benny is out there nodding at Mr. Aikens over the barbecue grill. Benny can con anybody. Standing there with his black hair combed out of his face and his hands in his pockets, nodding at Mr. Aikens, he looks as if he's never punched little kids in the throat for a nickel. Cling won't be here; he dropped out of school "in first grade," he says. Behind Benny, I see Keith Gurber talking to the Starkey twins. They're all drinking orange soda pop. Max has one hand in the air, flattened as a plane, turning real slow figure eights. Keith is transfixed.

Before I can get out of the kitchen, Karen Wilkes turns from where she's been filling bowls with potato chips with Josie Herron and says, "Larry. What have you been doing all summer?"

I look in her sweet face, one of my favorite faces in the

whole grade school, and I utterly believe that I have been seeing her all summer and she hasn't seen me once. Her eyes are large and round and her upper lip flips up a little. It makes her look like she's always about to flirt.

"Not much, Karen," I say. I remember everything I've ever said to her. "Playing baseball." I look at her smile and remember seeing her shorts twisting over Parley's hand, but I don't trust the moment or the memory. This is absolute stupid puberty. I grin and nod. I actually grin and I actually nod.

Girls are always older than you; you can never catch up enough to know them well. Before I can embarrass myself, Mrs. Aikens takes my arm and says she wants to show me where the soft drinks are. She takes me in the bright yellow utility room right across from the kitchen.

"Well?" Mrs. Aikens says.

"It's a nice room."

"No, Larry, do you know where the soft drinks are?"

"In the fridge?"

"No!" She laughs and laughs at this. I kind of smile. She recovers and says, "No, no, no. Here they are! Presto!" She opens the lid of the washing machine and I see that it's full of ice. "What would you like?"

"Is there any cream soda?" I'm just going along

with her all the way.

She reaches into the washing machine and extracts a tall bottle of Nehi Creme Soda. "And here's the opener." It's dangling on a string above the washer. "I read about this trick in Party Hints in the paper. Of course, you have to unplug the washer to be safe." She bends and shows me the three-prong washer plug as proof that we're safe.

"That's a great idea, Mrs. Aikens," I say, hoping she'll just hand me the soda and let me go. "I certainly wouldn't have thought of that."

"Yes, well, a good party starts with good planning."

Finally she awards me the cream soda and we step back into the kitchen, and I'm able to fade out into the backyard. Linda Aikens is in the corner of the patio, adjusting the speaker cords behind some wicker furniture.

"Hi, Linda."

"Larry!" She pushes a chair into place and turns to smile at me. "Oh, I'm glad you came!" And you know, the way she says it is right: she means it. She's parted her dark hair in a new way, right down the middle, real tight and shiny, and the rest of her hair is pinned up in two braids. She kind of looks like Heidi in the movie.

I hold up my soda. "In the washer. You want one?"

"No, I want to get the music lined up. Will you dance with me later?"

The backyard is hard to figure out. There is another lamppost on one side gathering bugs in a busy halo, and a tall hedge surrounds the whole thing. The lawn is great; it just makes you want to practice a few slides. They're not storing anything out here: any lumber, a wheelbarrow, or even an old boat. The yard is filling up with kids, but it still seems like such a waste, all that thick lawn. I say hello to Mr. Aikens, who looks pretty young to be somebody's father. He's got freckles on his forehead. "You guys all know each other?" he says to us, and I say, "Yes, we do." Benny gives me a sly look. I'm mainly trying to do the three things my mother told me: stand straight up; not drink my soda in four gulps; not hang around the potato chips. Rafferty is hanging around the potato chips. Evidently, his mother didn't talk to him.

For a while Mr. Aikens is serving everybody hot dogs, and Mrs. Aikens is showing everybody the washing machine. Then Linda puts on some music, and kids start dancing on the cement patio. It's mainly the bigger guys, Torkelson and Kidder, guys who have already spent the summer chasing girls, unafraid of having girlfriends.

I watch the kids dance for a while and then, between

songs, I stand up and take my paper plate back into the kitchen. Though I made my soda last longer than any in the history of my life, it has been empty for half an hour. The bottle's warm. No one is in the kitchen except two girls, who are leaning over the sink to look out the window at the dancers. Turning into the utility room, I bump into Mrs. Aikens. I show her the empty bottle and make a friendly gesture toward the washer, but she's taking another bag of chips outside, and so I am spared a second tour and simply help myself to another cold bottle of cream soda.

"I haven't seen you dance yet." Linda has come up behind me on the lawn. "Are you ready?"

"Sure, I'm ready." The party has continued easily through the evening. I've mainly been experimenting with new ways to hold my soda so as not to warm it up so much with my hand. I've watched Rafferty move to three stations, each beside a recently filled potato chip bowl, and stuff his face. Tomorrow there's going to be a triangular trail in the lawn from his feeding pattern. For a few minutes Grant and Max and some guys started having chicken fights, riding piggyback all over the yard, but Mrs. Aikens stopped that. She rushed out and asked Max, who was riding on Grant's shoulders, if he was all right.

It took the spirit out of it for them, I guess, because they all settled down and headed for the washing machine.

But mostly it has been couples dancing, doing the twist and the hop and a little of the pony, and once Linda and Karen led four other girls in the stroll, which looked real smooth and ancient, like a dance they'd known forever. I thought, How do they know how to do these things? And now I stand with Linda Aikens, one arm on her hip, the other in her hand, the way I was taught, as the next song begins. I look over at Keith and he smiles at me. He's a kid just happy to be organizing the music. He hasn't had to drop any pamphlets in the river or have his friends ask if he studies dirty magazines.

The song is "Earth Angel" and as it starts, I commence the two-step as instructed by Mr. Compton, but instead of it becoming the stepping and steering activity I'd known last year, this dance changes. Just as I was groping through my mind to initiate conversation, Linda's head collapses against my chin. For a minute I think I might have to carry her to a chair. But no, she's moving, she's all right, she's just moving slowly in microscopic shuffle steps. I think: I can do this. For a while I concentrate hard on not kicking her over as I stare out on the lawn where my half bottle of cream soda stands alone.

Then, without trying, I've got it. Linda's forehead, the very start of her part, is against the corner of my mouth, and though I try to stand up straight, I soon find my head against her head that way as we dance. Evidently there will be no conversation. I had practiced asking her if she was going to registration on Tuesday, but the sentence vanishes. And that feels wonderful, the vanishing, because this dancing becomes the easiest thing I have ever done. We are inventing something powerful here. As the song ends, I peel my face from Linda's forehead; sweat has stuck us together.

Linda says "Just a minute" to me and goes over to give Keith some help. While I'm standing on the edge of the patio, Rafferty calls my name, and I watch him walk over and gently toe my soda over onto its side. He smiles at me as if he's just done a classic party stunt. I look at his new chrome glasses and red shirt, and I swear I don't know him anymore.

I don't really even know where I am or what I'm doing, but Linda is back, taking my hand, pulling me through the dancers, off the patio, around the redwood trellis, into the darkness of the side yard. We can hear the music start: "Poetry in Motion." When Linda stops, I almost run into her. The sweat in the fringe of her hair is reflected in the starlight.

"Did you get my note?"

"Yeah," I say. She is still holding my hand. "I did."
Maybe this is the conversation, but she doesn't say anything, just looks up at me, so I add, "I found it in my
book."

I hear the part of the song I like, that neat rhyme
motion and *ocean*. Linda looks up at me with a look I've
never seen anybody make, not even in movies, and she
lifts her arms around my neck and pulls herself up as I
reach down and we kiss. I don't know if it is a long or a
short kiss, just that she is against me, her lips against
mine, and when I place my arms around her back, one of
my hands flattens on her bra and I move that hand. I look
once and see her eyes are closed.

Then she stands back down on her heels and smiles
at me, looks at the ground, lets go of my hand, and walks
back around to the party. The first thing I do when she
leaves is look around to see if anybody saw us; then I
realize I am not going back to the party. I can do everything there is to do, dance, find soda in the washing
machine, stand up straight, not gobble the potato chips,
but I cannot walk back around that trellis and have
Rafferty smile at me again with his big, fake face. What I

do is look at my shoes.

I find the redwood gate in the side yard, which is six feet tall, but I can't work the old latch, so I pull and scramble up and finally place a foot on top of it to climb over. But, with one of my legs still hanging and kicking, the gate starts to swing open. I can't do anything but ride it around until it stops against the house, and I find myself looking in the bathroom window. Karen Wilkes is sitting in there knee to knee with Linda, who is perched on the tub, and they are talking like two maniacs planning an escape. Linda has her hands over both of her ears as if to hold her head together, I guess, and, though I can't hear a word they say, it is the one time in my life when I am sure that somebody is talking about me.

10 the white plate

In deciduous broad leaves, the green pigment chlorophyll breaks down in autumn when evening temperatures descend. This allows other pigments to emerge, such as xanthophyll, which is yellow, and carotene pigments, which are orange-red.

I have seen Witt almost every day this whole summer, even slept out with him over fifty-four times, and now I don't see him for a week. In fact, I don't see anybody, really. With Little League over, no one is ever in the park. Rafferty, I know, has other interests, and Witt may be in Idaho. My mother has already bought my school clothes and a new backpack and binder and a sheaf of lined paper. It's like a thousand pages of paper; she has such high hopes for me. I want to tell everybody that if they think they're smart for considering summer over, they've jumped the gun. It's still summer; it just tastes different. The light has fallen away afternoons, and the neighborhood is run with shadows. Then the day arrives when I have to go over to the junior high and register, and I enter the same holding pattern that the whole neighborhood has assumed.

My mother asks if I want her to go to the big new school with me and I say no, that's all right. I go over alone, and it turns out the worst part is walking up to the doors. There are three rooms for registration. I don't see Witt in any of them. Rafferty shows up after a while with Kidder and some other guys I don't know, and he and I just nod at each other. I make up my mind to find out what is happening with Witt; I'll go down there tonight. From the second-story room in which I sign up for Algebra I, I can see the front playground sloping down to the bushes that line the river. Monumental weeping willows stand above them and trail in the water; and there, down from the walk bridge, is that one dead tree with the bra hanging in it like an insult.

After we register, the new students are sent to the cafeteria, the biggest room I've ever seen in a school. We sit at long tables on neat little stools that swing out on metal arms. When they pass out the four-page "diagnostic test," it all seems a lot like school, but the questions are fairly silly, such as "Do you like rain?" and "Are you afraid of the dark?" All you have to do is fill in the yes and no boxes with dark and heavy pencil marks. Witt would like this.

At the end there are three questions that ask you to write short answers. The last question is to describe something you do well, your main talent.

I lean forward, putting my head on my fist, three inches from where the answer is supposed to go. What do I do well? I want to write "play Wall Ball," but that would take too much explanation. I actually think my main talent is riding my bike all around, looking down from time to time at the handlebars and reading my name on the wristband of my old brown baseball mitt. Finally I just write "second base" and let it go. Witt would have so much to write on that question; he could really baffle the testers.

When I return home that afternoon, Eddie is down in our basement room, sprawled on the bed. His face is all flushed and cried out, and his lower lip is still vibrating.

"What happened?"

"Nothing."

The word chills me. "Come on, what happened?"

He shakes his head and turns back toward the wall. It's something you don't want to see: your brother home crying in the middle of the day. Witt has crying figured out; he wouldn't have any trouble with this.

"Did Cling and those guys pick on you?"

"We were down by the swings."

"Did he scare you?"

"Yeah." He starts crying a little again.

"Did he hit you?"

Eddie's quiet for a minute and then whispers, "I don't know." I look at him curled on the bed and I realize how much like me he really is. He doesn't know, he says. Well, I know. Cling hit him, and the truth is it doesn't matter, because I saw and dreaded this all summer, and now it's different than I expected because I'm mad down in my chest, hot and hurt for my brother, and it looks like the first fight of my life is going to be with Cling after all.

"You gonna be all right?" I say to Eddie.

"I'm okay." His voice is thick and hoarse from the crying, and it trebles the pain in my chest. I turn on the wall radio to try to make things normal, and the song is "Poetry in Motion." My emotions swirl like some vile mixture in a science fiction movie: vapor could come out my ears. I've been kissed. I've been inside the junior high. And then this Cling. The front of the radio seems the same as always, but life isn't simple anymore.

My mother intercepts me on the way out of the house. She wants to know where I am going, and adds, "I don't want you going down to Witt's today. Remember what we talked about: it's important to have more than one friend. School's starting soon."

This woman, this dear woman. She deserves a better son. I love my mother, but could I tell her I've been kissed, or that in two months I've become a nocturnal butt-looker who is addicted to the idiot songs on the radio? I don't tell her now that I am going out to find Cling and instruct him to leave my brother alone, that essentially I am going out to die. "I'm just going over to the park."

The park is empty. Two kids are up on the old rest room roof, tearing off pieces of tarpaper and throwing them up in loopy, flying saucer tosses. No one is swinging. No one is weaving boondoggle down on the bandstand; summer crafts has been over for a week. Someone has thrown an old kitchen chair onto the bandstand roof. I start circling the bandstand on my old green bike, counting the laps. When I was a little kid, they used to have bicycle races around this small track. My initials are carved in the bandstand a dozen times. I remember sitting up on the benches and watching the big guys race and race. Some of them had two bicycles and would change midway through. One kid named Gibson crashed one time and tore up his forehead and his knee. He sat on the lawn bleeding while the other cyclists went round and round. They seemed impossibly old, and now I am older than they were then. I don't see Cling.

Then I'm thinking about Linda Aikens and standing there with her in her yard and she's asking me if I received her note. I slow my bike and stagger to a stop on both feet. This is terrible. From out of nowhere I'm thinking about girls. It is the end of a world. I see Cling walk across the tennis courts and out of the park. I stand frozen. Then I look at my handlebars and start pedaling around the old bandstand. I do one hundred and ninety-one laps before I see my father's truck go by and my mother calls me home.

Dinner is a trial. My father is cheerful and keeps saying things like "When does school start?" and "You boys will be in different schools this year." I'm nodding and saying "Yeah," which my mother would spot as a bluff, but she's busy with Ricky. Eddie keeps his face down at his plate, but his eyes come my way several times. He's worried I'm going to mention Cling. I'm not going to mention anything. It's an old tactic of mine: say nothing and maybe the problem will go away. It hasn't been a great tactic.

Every night now I worry that the tennis court lights are not going to come on. I do not know who controls them or from where, but when they stop coming on, it's all over. They are summer. Tonight I'm down leaning on my bike against the stone drinking fountain when I see the courts fill with light, a tangible relief.

But then I see the unmistakable forms of Linda Aikens and Karen Wilkes walk into the glow. They fold their sweaters on the fence and begin playing tennis. The last thing I am able to think before my heart climbs through my throat is that girls have the ability at all times and in all places to be casual, and it is an amazing and enviable skill.

I cruise over and lean my bicycle on the lawn and walk to the edge of the light.

"Hi, Larry!" Karen says. Linda is back shagging the ball. In a minute Karen is shagging, and Linda says, "Oh, hi." They may be casual, but they still can't play tennis. Every ten minutes they hit the ball two times consecutively, but then—in the heat of that excitement—the third stroke usually goes over my head fifty feet, so I get to do some shagging too. What amazes me is that they act as if they are having fun. What could be the fun part? I stand there watching them attempting to play tennis, and realize there's a whole lot of stuff going on that I know nothing about.

When a family arrives to play doubles on the other court, Karen and Linda interrupt that game so many times that the girls finally get weary of saying "Excuse me" and quit. We stroll over to the swings, the girls swinging their rackets, trimming the grass. I walk my bike.

"How'd you like the party the other night, Larry?" Karen asks me. We all sit on the swings and drag our feet.

"It was fun. I enjoyed it."

"Where'd you disappear to?"

"Oh, yeah, I had to get home early. But it sure was a nice party." Karen has a way of talking that makes you feel she knows everything already and always will. A little burn of sweat rises along my hairline: did they see me on the gate? I'm scrambling for things to say. I want to tell Linda that her mother actually said "Presto," but I settle for, "Your mother was smart to keep the sodas in the washer."

"My mother can be a pain," Linda says. "But the other night she was okay."

"Your dad's nice too."

"I never see him."

"Oh." The conversation falls from a cliff and hits the ground and rolls dead into its grave. I skim my tennis shoes on the sand, trying to make a real smooth area.

"Did you see any cute girls from Riverside or Northwest at the registration?"

"Not too many," I say. "There were a lot of people, though. How'd you like that test?"

"I hate tests!"

I've never really talked to girls before except to lend them an assignment or a pencil, and I'm finding that this is the hardest swinging in the park I've ever done. I've bailed out of all of these swings at their highest point and landed in the sweet sand with my ankles burning, but this sitting is tougher. The three of us are just barely swinging, back and forth. Now I'm making a design in the smooth area I paved with my foot: when I see it's my initial, I start all over again, consciously this time, on a star.

Linda looks beautiful. She's wearing a white shirt with no sleeves. Her arms are brown. They shine. Her hair is held up by a couple of red clips. I think to myself:

I've kissed her, but I look at her and I don't believe it. At all.

I take Linda's tennis racket and sift the sand a little bit, finding two Popsicle sticks. When the sand dissolves, there is a bright silver dime left on the strings.

"Look," I say, and Linda looks right in my face, starting my heart all over again. "It's for you."

"How sweet," Karen says. She stands up and wanders to the ladder of the slippery slide. She climbs to the top and then sits backward, her feet on the last rung. I'm wondering if girls have signals for these times, when one is supposed to walk away and climb the slippery slide so the other can whisper alone with the boy she kissed at the party. Seeing Karen sitting up there backward and wondering about their signals makes me feel funny; I have been in a thousand situations this summer, and I realize that I haven't fully understood what was going on in even one.

Linda picks the dime off the racket. "It is sweet," she says to me. And then she whispers, "I heard our song today." I don't know what to say to this. Our song? Then it comes into my heart: We have a song. I've never had a song before, and I'm in a spot. I'm in one of the great spots of my lifetime. This is worse than being caught flat-footed in the hot box between home and third. Linda Aikens has heard our song, and I don't know what it is. I look out into the park as if the tennis court lights with their million moths were the most important thing I have ever seen. I know I am not going to say, "What song would that be, Linda?" It's got to be "Earth Angel" or "Poetry in Motion." Do people have two songs? If it is the "Ba-bay, something, something" song, I'm hurting.

I catch a movement behind us, and I turn to see Cling walking slowly our way. He's come up out of the darkness like the Creature from the Black Lagoon. He is exactly what I don't want to see.

My heart, which has just started, stops. Forget the song problem. Here's Cling. I don't feel like bringing up the subject of my brother. I don't feel like asking Cling to stop picking on Eddie. In fact, I don't feel like being here swinging on the last night of summer with the girls. Cling advances.

"Playing in the sand?"

"Yeah, Cling."

"Playing with the girlies?"

I don't answer this. I try to laugh a little, but the chuckle twists, chokes me. Cling is not exactly looking at me. He's looking at Karen and Linda. His eyes are glassy and swollen.

"You know how to play with the girlies?"

"Oh, sure, Cling. We were just playing some tennis and now we're resting." I nod at him and look at the girls. The best thing they look is puzzled; the worst is real scared.

"Naa-oow," he groans and flips his cigarette at me. It bounces off my chest in a tiny splash of ashes and falls into the sand. I put my foot on it and then check that I'm not on fire. When the cigarette hits me, Linda gasps. Karen climbs down the slide ladder and comes over. "It's okay," I tell the girls. "Cling's just having fun."

And I think he is until he reaches in his pocket and pulls out a piece of pink cloth. "No, no!" Cling says, waving the cloth. "Girls want you to play with their pants!" He laughs and waves the cloth in my face. I see that it's a pair of panties. He steps across in front of me and grabs the chain of Linda's swing. "Right, girls?" Linda jumps away and he reaches for her, but he makes the mistake of grabbing my arm in his lurch. If he hadn't touched me, I might have spent the rest of the night, my knuckles frozen on the chains of my swing. But, somehow, it clears my throat. I can breathe. I remember him hitting my brother Eddie, and I grab his arm as hard as I can and pull him back in front of me.

There is no argument. I had kind of expected to tell him off or warn him or cry or complain or do something else that involved words, but I don't. I push him reflexively back two steps, and he throws the panties in my face, slaps me once in the neck, and begins pulling my head apart with his fingers. They are in my mouth pulling, and one thumb is above my eye, trying to gouge off the top of my head. I go down first and he falls on me with a knee on my chest. I'm kicking for balance, and I suck a lot of sand, but Cling doesn't hit me. When I reach up and seize his arms above the elbows, I'm surprised at how soft they are. He is still just prying my face off, not hitting me. I squeeze his arms and push and arch my back and thrust him sideways off me into the sand. He rises growling and smiling. He spits through his teeth at me. He comes at me in a stance that would only be effective if he had a club in his hands. I step into his charge, just like it was a slow pitch, and I swing my right fist into his mouth as hard as I can. I'm right-handed and it's like I know what I'm doing. From then on I lose track. I hit him seven or eight times straight. I fall on him and stroke him three times with my left fist while I hold his filthy hair in my right hand. When I hear myself crying, I stop hitting him and go over and lean against the slippery slide. Neither one of us has said a word.

The girls are gone. Linda has left her tennis racket in the sand and I pick it up. Cling puts his hand in front of his face, thinking I'm going to hit him with it. I consider it for a minute, just one solid forehand to the nose, but he's all bloody, and it's not my racket.

What I really ache to do is to step on his head, put a foot on each of his ears, so he'd understand that it's no fun, that it's rude, crude, and ignorant. What I do is point at him once and say quietly, "You leave my little brother alone or I'll find you again and kick your ass." I couldn't have said it if I hadn't pointed, and when I hear the words as they come into the world, it is strange: I absolutely believe them. They feel like the first thing I've ever said.

It must have been during the long, heady run along the river, across the junior-high schoolyard, over the walk bridge to Linda's house, that I became an adolescent. As I lean the tennis racket against her front door and skip back into the cool darkness, I don't know what is going on, what has been going on, or what I am going to do next. I say "Kick your ass!" again, and it feels so good to say. "Kick your ass." Yet, unlike all the confusions I've ever felt, this one comes in a rush, a wonderful rush of welling happiness and black despair. I can feel it in my arms and legs; I can do anything. I'm on fire. Instead of the world being out there, it is here now, under my feet as I run back, and I am in the center. I stop on the walk bridge and breathe deeply from the river of air coming down the greenish dark corridor of willows over the water. My skin is hot in the damp air and my eyes are open to everything that catches light. My eyes feel electric. I raise my arms: I can do anything. I'm upset, I think: This is being upset. "Here I am," I say aloud. And then, "I'll kick your ass!" When I get home, I'll wake Eddie up and tell him Cling won't bother him anymore. I see now that the knuckles on my right hand are bleeding, and I suck at them and wipe them on my pants.

I stand on the bridge and think: Here is a man with a song. It doesn't bother me so much that I don't know what it is. So what if I hear "Poetry in Motion" and have the feelings, and then it turns out to be the wrong song? The truth is that right now all songs are mine, even every "ba-bay, ba-bay," and they all thicken my throat and go to my knees. The river runs steadily beneath me, and I know that finally I have a firm grasp of music, the purpose of all music in the universe.

My head clears, my knuckles burn and drum, and I realize that I am going to get that bra out of that tree. That bra shouldn't be there, and I'm the guy. I leave the bridge and walk down around onto the overgrown bank. Somewhere behind me, I can hear our waterwheel moaning low, still measuring the speed of the water. Then I'm hopping through the brush along the river; the tangled jungle reaches for me in the dark, but soon I find a clearing and search for the tree. Shadows outnumber things. It is as still as sleep in here. To reach the bra tree I have to climb over a clump of wild stickers, and they line my forearms with hot scratches. The bark is rotten, but by using the vines, I pull myself up to the dead part of the tree.

The river reflects itself sheetwise beneath me, and I can see quiet, silver sections of it running through the trees all the way around the school.

The bra hangs twenty feet above me on a finger-thin limb.

The roof of the junior high looks like the map of a strange new world, each section claiming a new country. I think of Rafferty and how he's changed, and of Witt, and I wonder if he is dropping out of school; I think of Linda Aikens and the school dances coming up. I wonder what Witt would think if he knew I fought Cling, if he could

270

see me now. I know what he'd think. He'd say: That's it. Those are the things you do; you've finally got it.

I look up. The barkless dead branches above me are round and smooth as bones. I move up them surely, carefully, my arms and legs wrapped around each branch. From here I can see all the way back to the park. Witt was right; it's up here that time lives. The tennis court lights are still on, but the courts are empty. I see a car two blocks away on Derby pull into a driveway and turn off its lights as if on command. From here the whole world I know resembles the late-summer set for someone else's life.

I hear myself singing, and I see you don't really need to know the words or believe them; they ride through me like something, something.

Using my knees, I pull upward to thinner branches, higher in the sky. The branches are thinner than I thought, and the whole brittle section vibrates. I'm climbing a skeleton. I reach for the bra, tug at the end, and lose my hold. For a second I am slipping. My head lifts away from my body, swirling. I slide down and catch at a Y of branches. For several ten-gallon breaths, I sit there like a soul arriving on Earth by way of the trees, my legs bowed out in a wishbone. The feeling is rich and dizzy. I think, Why do this? Scanning the planet turning quietly below me, I decide there's an answer to that question; I just don't know it.

Then I feel it. I've been groping this tree so intensely that my crotch feels strange, a little ache, a little heat. My cutoffs are all bunched and I'm surprised by this erection; it feels like a bruise and is growing. For pete's sake. I climb back up, up on a limb as big as my arm, like a man on a flagpole, and grab the bra firmly in my fist. Right between the cups. The ache in my groin doubles. I pull at the bra, but it won't let go and the antlered branches above me chatter in the night. Now, suddenly, the ache runs electric in my crotch and I reach down to cup myself with the other hand, arching against the limb to ease the strange burning; and when I do, the waving pain breaks so brightly that I say a word that goes into the sky, and the limb explodes like a gunshot, and I am falling now for real, flying backward, stock still in air and then down to the night glass of the river. I smack the river and its bottom simultaneously, it seems. Is it only this deep? Plunging one foot in the spongy mud, leaving the shoe, I kick upward still holding on to my pennant, the bra. I break the surface and scramble ashore, flabbergasted, as my mother would say. I stand up and then sit down and breathe and breathe. I'm trembling. "Here," I say aloud, and I wave the bra and throw it in the river. "Here." I feel my cutoffs and adjust myself, happily. What a fake out. I didn't know this would happen. Nobody said anything about being in trees.

From the walk bridge I look down at the changing broad slip of the river. The huge shadow of the junior high reaches out in the starlight. It is my new school. There is a nice chill in the air, and many groups of early leaves float by, under me. The wind sucks a little at my wet shirt. I peel it off and wring it out, something all wet adolescents should do. More leaves blow past, forming little fleets on the water. My eyes well up for no reason.

It's late, but I've got to see Witt, find him, find out what's going on, where he's been. I lope down to Witt's, one shoe on, one shoe lost. My mind races as I think of what I am going to tell my mother. What'd you do with that shoe? Nothing, none of your business! It's my shoe! I laugh like a madman. I am a madman. Oh, I love my mother. Where's your shoe, Larry? Locked forever in river mud, Mother! Along with your crazy sex pamphlet! And do you now what else has happened? I laugh and laugh, confused right to the linings of my heart, but loving each assault of fear and crazy happiness. Laughing and saying words, I limp all the way down the high, rough crown of Concord Street.

The last time I saw Witt, the day after the all-star game, he told me that Atom had disappeared. I said, "Oh, he'll be back," because Atom has disappeared all summer for days at a time.

"No, he's gone this time," Witt said. "We won't see that dog anymore." Witt wouldn't tell me what he meant. The dog was gone. In a funny way I had come to think of Atom as my dog. He is the only dog in the neighborhood I know by name; I think he is the only dog that had a name. For a few days after that, when I was riding to the store or down to Rafferty's, I looked for him. I even poked around some of the trash in the vacant lots, thinking he might be passed out somewhere or sleeping off something he had eaten, but Witt was going to be right about Atom. He had disappeared. "When we see that dog again, he'll be something else," Witt said. A few birds dipped over our heads and Witt pointed at them. "He might come back as a bird or as one of the kids who will move into the old Casey house." I remember I had felt it that day: Atom is gone. I had looked up at those three birds and they were the right color, but none of them, not one, looked like

Atom. I looked for the little letters on their sides. I could see a white spot on each, but that was all.

Witt's house is dark. There isn't any light from the kitchen, where someone has usually left the fridge open, nor is there any noise coming out of the hole in the corner of the house where Bud smashed into it. As I slip along the driveway, there is a clatter from under the old Hudson and I freeze and kneel slowly. In the patchy dark underneath the car, I can't see a thing, and then light takes a profile that slowly clarifies itself into the bumpy forehead of Ferguson, the alligator. I'm sure it's him. Neither of us moves. Our glances hold; he knows all about me.

In the backyard, there is a steady rage of crickets. I feel my way around the geothermal pit, and I see a dim light in the bushes.

"Hey!" I whisper.

"Over here."

He's sleeping way out back, hidden in the weeds in a little-explored portion of the lot. He's made a camp, in fact, with two milk crates, one of them full of apples, and a bag of bread, and three cans of VanCamp's pork and beans. There are books and papers and a few bags and gizmos spread around. Lazy, the yellow cat, is curled on the tattered end of Witt's sleeping bag. I can tell by the way the weeds are matted that Witt's been here for a few nights. He shines his flashlight on me. He runs it up and down my half-wet clothing and focuses on my one bare foot. I know he won't ask me about it.

"Well, how was the class party?" Beside him on the ground is his big duffel bag, stuffed full. He's out of his life. There's a dirty white cast on his left arm from wrist to elbow.

"What are you doing, Witt? You going for a new sleep-out record?"

"You could say that," he says, climbing out of his sleeping bag. I'm glad to see him. It's a relief and makes me feel a little like my old self.

I point at the duffel bag. "You going on a trip?"

"Always," he says. "Look at this." He speaks that sentence the same old way, lost in a new experiment. I can see his face is different, lopsided, his left jaw shadowed and dirty or swollen. He extracts a roll of papers from a cardboard tube as if nothing is wrong and spreads them on his sleeping bag, weighing down the corners with cans of pork and beans. "This is my house. See the school?" He can move his arm real well, and with his dirty fingers he traces the blue lines. "The river. Your house. The park; this is the bandstand. I've got the elevations, too; the river is thirteen feet below where we stand right now."

It is by far the prettiest map I've ever seen. He's drawn it all with a blue pencil, and it is thrilling just to look at it. A map. I sit back on my heels and fold my arms; I've kind of collapsed. My eyes burn faintly and I feel a sore above my right elbow. I must have hit something coming out of that tree.

"Did you register for school?" I say to Witt. "Are you okay?"

He rolls the map, taps the end straight, and inserts it in the tube. "Okay? I'm mapping the world."

"Witt," I start. "With school starting and all . . ." I nearly say, *Don't your parents want you to go to school?* Then I see the whole picture. Witt has moved out of his house. He's moved out; he's not going to school anymore, and he's mapping the world.

"We've had a little difficulty down here," he says. He shoves the map tube into a milk crate and goes over to Haslams' fence, and I follow. The crickets in our path are bold, having never seen human beings before, and they barely stop roaring for a moment while we pass. Witt leans against the abandoned refrigerator, his back to me.

"Where you going?" I ask him.

"You probably got a lot to do at the new school, I

mean with all your new friends, girls to chase."

"There are a lot of kids, Witt. You'd like it."

He turns his head slowly to me and says, "I'd like it." It's a voice I've never heard before. He runs the flashlight into my eyes and steps over to me real close, reaching into my hair and picking out a little section of willow that is tangled there. His palm is on the side of my face, and then he wipes something from my cheek and drops the light.

"Well, it's going to be good, meeting the new kids." I don't know what to say, so this comes out, "It's good, it's okay to have more than one friend."

"Right," he says softly in the dark, and turns back away from me, but it's too late. I could see in the dirt on his face that he is crying, and his voice tells the whole story. "Witt, what's the matter? Hey?" But when I approach him, he pushes off the fridge and walks past me to his camp. "Witt?"

"I'm going up to Pocatello for a while."

"Pocatello? To your uncle's? You were just up there."

"Well, I'm going back. I get Idaho and Budd gets therapy. He breaks my arm and he gets the therapy."

He reaches in a milk crate and holds out a paper bag. I take it. Inside are all my bottle-cap men. They've been down here for a long time.

I take out a green plastic cap. That guy could really hit. Some of these guys, I realize, are six years old.

Now Witt has covered his face in both hands. I stand in the crickets and watch his back for two minutes.

"Witt? Witt, are you okay?"

He whispers, "My days of tormenting Budd are over. I've been told."

"Is your uncle's a good idea?"

"Go away, Larry," he says finally. "Go home."

I limp halfway home on that one shoe until I pass the monstrous poplar in front of Lopez's. I stand there and throw my shoe up into the tree three, four, five times until it catches. I toss my dirty socks into the vacant lot. There, too, I bury the bottle caps. While I kneel and dig in the dirt, I smell the neighborhood, the trees, the weeds, sweet acrid ashes of Mr. Wilkes's fire.

I look up. A figure rises across the weedy meadow.

"Parley?" I say. My eyes sting with fatigue and I can't see clearly. "Parley?"

The figure wavers in the darkness, lifts a hand, shimmers on the surface of my eyes, and disappears. There is no one there. As I stand to scan the vacant lot, the tennis court lights across the street in the park go out. It's late.

I remember the first time I met Witt. We were in the first grade, Miss Scanlon's class, and we were paired up on an autumn leaf project. We were in charge of taping yellow leaves we'd gathered onto the side bulletin board in a large circle. "I know what makes them change color," he told me. He held up a beauty, half green and half yellow, and it was the first spark for me. I thought, There are reasons for things? He asked me how old I was and I lied: I said six. After school, we walked down the block to his house and he showed me an experiment. He heated a white dinner plate on the kitchen stove and ran it outside in an old towel. When he poured cold water on the plate, it cracked into three pieces.